Out of Nowhere

Teresa Roman

Dedicated to my little loves,
I never knew true happiness until I met you

Chapter 1
Dress Shopping

There was no point in denying it any longer. I was jealous of my best friend. As Jessica stepped out of the fitting room in the dress I knew she'd choose as her wedding gown, I was so green with envy I felt like a freaking tropical rainforest.

It wasn't because she looked absolutely stunning in the form-fitting sheath dress she had on, or even the fact that she was going to be married in two weeks. It was because I could tell how deeply and madly in love she was with her fiancé, Justin. And how happy she was. Something I hadn't been for a long time.

Jesse did a quick spin so I could see the back of her dress. "What do you think?" she asked.

Just as quickly as my jealousy had reared its ugly head, it slunk away, tail between its legs. Jesse deserved to be happy, and truthfully, I was excited for her. If anyone had earned their happily-ever-after, it was Jesse. I stood up and stared at her, appreciating the intricate beading that accentuated the bodice of her dress. "You look amazing," I said, smiling. "That dress is perfect."

She turned to look in the mirror, studying her reflection. "I think this is the one." Her voice trembled with excitement.

"I had a feeling you'd say that."

"You don't like it?"

"No. I love it," I replied. "It's beautiful."

Jesse peered over her shoulder. "When are we going dress shopping for your wedding?"

"As soon as Greg and I set a date," I said, hoping her next question wasn't going to be 'and when is that going to happen?' since that had truly become the most annoying question on the face of this earth.

Jesse studied my expression for a moment before asking, "Sue, is there something you're not telling me?"

"What do you mean?"

"You and Greg have been engaged for almost two years and still haven't set a date. I know you keep telling me everything's fine, but there's got to be a reason."

There was and there wasn't, but I didn't really know how to explain it, so there was no use trying. Not long after Greg proposed he lost his job. For weeks he sat on the couch drinking beer and watching sports. We began arguing. I grew tired of watching him wallow in self-pity and he grew tired of my nagging. Eventually all my pushing and shoving got Greg off the couch, and he finally managed to find another job. But all our arguing had taken a toll on our relationship. The spark wasn't there anymore, no matter how hard I kept hoping it would come back. Couples went through ups and downs all the time, and despite everything, we were still engaged. Although sometimes I wasn't sure that I wanted to be. Or that I didn't want to be. I hated admitting it to myself, but truthfully, I really had no idea what I wanted anymore, and that was why, despite being engaged for almost two years, I had no wedding date to announce.

"I just don't want to rush into anything. That's all. And weddings cost money." Neither Greg nor I had the kind of money Jesse's future in-laws did.

"If there was something else going on, you'd tell me, right?" Jesse said, her voice full of concern.

"Of course I would," I replied, although I wasn't really sure that was true. Jesse and I were such good friends that in some ways I saw myself as her sister—her much older sister. Being almost ten years older than Jesse meant that I was supposed to have my shit together and be there for her when she came to me for advice, not the other way around, which worked out, because as an only child I'd always wanted a kid sister.

"I'm going to get changed," Jesse said. "You want to grab lunch?"

"Sure."

She walked back inside the fitting room and emerged a few minutes later with the dress she'd just tried on draped over one arm.

"You do know that your soon-to-be mother-in-law would just die if she knew you were buying an off-the-rack wedding dress," I said as we walked over to the register to pay for it.

"I don't exactly have time for a custom made gown. And you said it yourself, this dress is perfect." Even though Jesse was about to marry into a wealthy family, she was still the same old Jesse. I was happy that money hadn't turned her into a different person. "Besides what Allison doesn't know can't hurt her."

We had lunch at a nearby deli, nothing fancy, just a place where you could get a good Italian sub and a soda. As we sat down, Jesse reached into her purse and pulled out an envelope.

"I almost forgot to give you this." It was an invitation for the wedding shower Allison Lambert was throwing for her son, Justin, and soon-to-be daughter-in-law. I ripped open the seal and skimmed through the note written in fancy calligraphy, even though Jesse had filled me in on the details of the party a few weeks ago.

"I still think you should let me throw you a bridal shower-slash-bachelorette party instead."

When I'd floated that idea to Jesse a few weeks ago she'd turned me down. Neither she nor Justin wanted to do the bachelor or bachelorette party thing.

"Allison really wanted to do this and I couldn't say no."

"Don't worry about it," I reassured her. "I totally understand."

"So you don't mind me hijacking your whole weekend?"

I'd almost forgotten that the day before her wedding shower was supposed to be another shopping day. This time for maid of honor and bridesmaid dresses.

"Like I have anything else to do," I said, only partly joking.

Jesse and I had both graduated with degrees in education a little over four months ago. Since then I'd been studying for my teacher certification exam, which I'd passed a few weeks ago. With college behind me, and no full-time job yet, I had too much time on my hands.

Jesse smiled. "It's going to be a lot of fun."

I didn't doubt that was true. I'd only been to the Lamberts' place once after Allison threw a graduation party for Jesse last spring, and talk about fancy. But an extravagant rooftop deck party wasn't the only reason to look forward to going to the Lamberts. The other was it meant I'd get a chance to see Justin's hotter-than-hot younger brothers, Jeff and James, again.

After lunch, Jesse and I parted ways at the train station. She lived in Manhattan with Justin now, and I still lived in the same apartment in Bay Ridge that I had for the past seven years. Jesse and I had been friends for four of those years. We went to college together, and had taken a lot of the same classes, which was how we became friends. We used to see each other all the time, not only because we bumped into each other at school, but because she lived only a short train ride away in Cobble Hill. But things were different now that we were done with school.

After climbing the two flights of stairs to get to my walk-up apartment, Bailey, my golden retriever, jumped up on me with his tail wagging. It put a smile on my face. Having him greet me like that never got old. I heard the sounds of another sports broadcast coming from the TV, which meant Greg was home. Once upon a time he actually got off the couch on weekends so we could do fun things together. It felt like forever since the two of us had actually gone out on a date. These days he spent a lot of time at work, which was weird, since Greg had never really been the overachieving type, but I figured he was putting in all those extra hours because he was afraid of losing another job. Whenever I tried to talk him into going somewhere together, he'd complain that he was too tired. Lately, work and our couch were the two places he spent most of his time. Some nights he even fell asleep in front of the TV instead of joining me in bed.

"Suzie Q, is that you?" he called to me.

"Yup, it's me," I said as I walked into the living room.

He looked over his shoulder. "You're home sooner than I thought you'd be. Isn't wedding dress shopping supposed to be an all-day thing?"

"You know Jesse. She's not high maintenance. I think she tried on all of three gowns before she found the one she wanted."

Greg's attention had already turned back to the game. I still had a few things to say, like, when is it going to be my turn to try on wedding dresses? Were we ever going to set a date? Did he even want to get married anymore, or had he, like me, started to have doubts? Despite the questions that ran through my mind, I kept my mouth shut, not sure I was ready for that conversation. I used to be good at speaking my mind, but somehow I'd turned into a coward who couldn't work up the nerve to figure out what the hell she wanted from her life anymore.

On Monday morning I woke up to the screech of my alarm clock. I lay in bed for a few minutes trying to remember why I'd set it in the first place. Then I remembered I had a job subbing for an eighth-grade English class for the next two days. Since graduating I'd gotten out of the habit of waking up so early.

I quickly showered, dressed, finished a bowl of cereal, and gave Greg a kiss on the cheek before heading for the train station. Despite having to wake up so early, I was grateful whenever I got a substitute teacher gig. It paid decently and would improve my prospects of landing a full-time teaching position, which I desperately needed, because no matter how much I loved doing it, the money I made from subbing and my weekend dog-walking business wasn't enough.

Another sub job later in the week would've been nice, but it didn't happen, leaving me stuck at home in front of the computer job-hunting for the rest of the week. By the time the weekend rolled around I was eager to get out of the house. I loved Bailey, but sometimes I missed human company. Jesse's upcoming wedding had become a welcome distraction from my relationship and job woes.

On Saturday morning I met Jesse at Macy's in downtown Brooklyn right as it opened. Jesse's sister-in-law, Melanie, who'd gotten married to Jesse's brother over the summer, joined us. Sophia, one of Justin's cousins, also came along. The two of them were going to be bridesmaids. I could tell by the look on Sophia's face that she did not approve of Jesse's casual approach toward wedding planning, or the fact that her bridal party's dresses weren't going to match. Unlike Sophia I could care less about matching, or that we were buying bridesmaids dresses from a department store, I just thought Jesse was crazy to wait until a week before her wedding. But between all of our different schedules, this was the one time we could all get together.

Since it was autumn, Jesse wanted us to stick to a color palette that reflected the season. Other than that one request, she pretty much let us pick out what we wanted.

"I've never heard of someone picking out bridesmaids' dresses like this," I heard Sophia say to someone on her cell phone as she tried on a dress in the fitting room next to mine. "I mean, we're not even at a bridal shop. We're at freaking Macy's."

Despite her whining, she managed to find a dress she liked. Mel and I did, too. My dress was knee-length, forest green with thick straps, and a V-neck collar. Mel picked something in a pumpkin color, and Sophia chose a deep scarlet dress. When the three of us stood beside each other, I had to admit Jesse's vision was pretty spot-on. We looked like the colorful autumn leaves on the trees that lined the streets of the city. Even Sophia seemed pleased by the way things were turning out.

"If we wind up not finding any teaching jobs I say the two of us go into business together as wedding planners," I joked after changing back into my clothes.

"We just might have to do that," Jesse said. "I've already sent out like a million resumes and I haven't even gotten one call for an interview. Maybe I should just join you walking dogs."

"Yeah, right. It's not like you're going to need the money."

"I know, but I want to make my own money, not live off of Justin's."

That was Jesse. The girl had more pride than almost anyone I knew, which was probably one of the reasons she wasn't going overboard with her wedding. In a total break from tradition, Justin and his family were pretty much paying for the whole thing, and I knew that made Jesse feel awkward. She would have preferred a much more low-key affair, with only a handful of guests in attendance, but she wanted to make everyone happy, namely Allison Lambert. Pleasing her in-laws meant a lot to her. Jesse's crappy parents had practically disowned her when she was a teenager, and like most of her extended family, lived in Croatia. Her brother would be the only family member to attend her wedding—I knew that had to be painful.

Suddenly I felt an urge to hug her right then and there in the middle of the Macy's dress department. I'd been so wrapped up in feeling jealous and sorry for myself that I'd forgotten about the fact that Jesse hadn't always had things easy. She truly deserved the happiness she'd found with Justin.

"You're not going to have to," I said, trying to sound sure of myself even though I really wasn't. "Because we're both going to find jobs."

After paying for our dresses, Sophia insisted that the four of us get coffee. The girl was a nonstop chatterbox, talking incessantly about how she didn't believe that Jesse could organize a wedding in such a short time and that she was sure our dresses would be a disaster because whoever heard of off-the-rack dresses for a wedding? Mel, Jesse, and I just sat there smiling, nodding, and sipping our coffee while Sophia prattled on.

When she excused herself to go to the bathroom, Jesse let out a sigh of relief.

"Everything okay?" Mel asked.

Jesse leaned back in her chair. "I just can't wait to get this wedding over with. Everyone's got an opinion about how Justin and I should be doing things. It's driving me crazy."

Mel laughed. "I totally know what you mean, girl. But you gotta remember one important thing. This is *your* wedding."

As the only unmarried one sitting there I didn't have much to offer to the conversation, so my mind wandered. Despite our problems, I didn't want to end things with Greg. I was tired of running from relationships when things got hard. All Greg and I needed was to get back to what we once had. When I'd suggested premarital counseling to him a few months ago he'd changed the subject. Perhaps if I brought it up again, he'd be more open to the idea. Once we talked things through then maybe the two of us could move forward and finally set a wedding date. Maybe by this time next year it would be my turn to walk down the aisle. If Jesse could make a wedding happen with just a few months of planning, so could I.

It was kind of crazy the way her wedding had come together. Justin had proposed less than four months ago when the two of them were in the Dominican Republic for her brother's wedding. Neither wanted a long engagement, so they were doing the impossible—having a New York wedding with only a few months of planning. I still couldn't believe that in another week my best friend was going to be married.

Chapter 2
Wedding Shower

Normally, I liked sleeping in on weekends, but the next morning I was too excited about going to Jesse's and Justin's wedding shower later to stay in bed. Despite the early hour, Greg was already up. I smelled coffee brewing, so I threw on my bathrobe and made my way over to our shoebox of a kitchen, where I found Greg standing in front of the stove scrambling eggs.

"I made coffee," he said, glancing over his shoulder as I joined him in the kitchen.

I beamed. "You're an angel." Without coffee I was barely functional. And since I was usually the one who brewed it, having it ready first thing in the morning was an unexpected treat. I grabbed the coffee pot and a mug from one of the cabinets and filled it. "Why are you up so early?" I asked.

"I'm going over to Brian's later to play cards and catch a football game."

I stared at his back, waiting for him to turn around and tell me he was kidding. When that didn't happen, I asked, "Did you forget about Jesse's party?"

Greg rotated the stove burner to the off position and let out a loud sigh. "You didn't really expect me to go, did you?"

"Yes, actually, I did. I'm Jesse's maid of honor and you're my fiancé, so yes, I expected you to come."

"You know I'm not any good at those stuffy parties," he said, reaching for a few plates from the cabinet next to him.

"It's not going to be stuffy," I insisted, already knowing he wouldn't change his mind without a fight, and I just wasn't in the mood. I knew what he'd say if I pushed—that he worked hard all week and wanted to relax on the weekends. "You know what? Just forget it; if you don't want to come, then don't. Although you could have at least told me sooner."

I slammed my mug down on the counter, turned around, and walked back to the bedroom, closing the door behind me. I sat on the edge of my bed, fuming.

A few minutes later Greg came in with a plate of eggs and toast in his hands. He held it out to me. "Don't be mad," he said.

I reigned in the sarcastic comment that was at the tip of my tongue. Greg never wanted to do things with me anymore. Sometimes it felt like we were more roommates than lovers. But he had made me breakfast *and* brought it to me, even though he knew I was upset. If he didn't care anymore, he wouldn't have done that.

I took the plate. "What am I going to tell Jesse when she asks why you're not there?"

"She knows how I am. I think she'd be more surprised if I went than if I didn't," he said with a roguish smile on his face.

That wasn't entirely true. Before Greg had lost his job he'd been a lot more outgoing. But something had happened to his confidence the day he got fired, and finding a new job hadn't repaired the damage. There was no point in bringing it up again, though, because the handful of times I had, Greg seemed convinced that everything was perfectly fine and that I was blowing things out of proportion.

"I just hope you don't flake out on me on her wedding day," I muttered.

"I wouldn't do that." Greg kicked the door shut and leaned down to give me a kiss. I rested the plate on the dresser. He kissed me again, this time more passionately. When he reached under my shirt, I realized he wanted to take me to bed, and though it had been a while, I just wasn't in the mood. I wanted to tell him that this wasn't a good time, that I was hungry, that I needed to walk Bailey. Although truthfully the real reason I didn't feel like making love was because I was disappointed that he'd chosen his friends over me. But he'd take it personally if I said no, even if I had a good reason, and I didn't want another fight. So I didn't tell him any of those things and instead let him undress me.

Greg took his time making love, seeming to savor every kiss and caress in a way he hadn't in a long time. He even lay beside me in bed afterward with his arms around me, instead of falling asleep or heading to the couch to watch TV. I ran my hands through his rust-colored hair, wondering why we didn't spend time like this with each other anymore. Maybe it meant the two of us were turning a corner.

Bailey's scratching at the door eventually pulled me out of bed. He needed his walk and so did the dogs I got paid to take care of on the weekends.

New York weather during autumn was always a crapshoot. Some years we'd wind up with stretches of warm, summer-like days, and other years it would be freezing by October. As luck would have it, this was one of those warm fall days. I wished Greg would've joined me, but he wasn't an animal lover. I had Bailey before the two of us started dating, and Greg had only begrudgingly accepted him as part of the package.

By the time I got back home, Greg had already left. I sighed, wondering if I was being too hard on him. Maybe my expectations were too high. He was a nice guy, after all. But every time I came home from work to find him with one hand wrapped around a beer bottle and the other around the remote, I had to wonder if I really wanted that to be the rest of my life. The resolve I'd had the day before to work things out with Greg had faded, and I was back to my former, doubt-filled state.

I had once told my mom about my misgivings, only to have her reply that at my age I didn't have a right to be that picky. Maybe she was right, at thirty-two I was almost the only unmarried female I knew. I'd never really cared that I'd chosen to do things differently from everyone else, but as I got older I began to question my decisions. Instead of going to college right after high school, I floated from one job to another, always just barely making ends meet. I'd also floated from boyfriend to boyfriend. It wasn't until a few years ago that I'd decided to get serious about my life. For a while I'd worked as a vet tech, but my salary didn't cover the high cost of living in New York, and I wasn't about to move, so I finally went to college to get a teaching degree because I loved the idea of working with kids. When I met Greg shortly after starting classes, it felt like the pieces of my life were finally falling in to place.

I hung Bailey's leash on the hook behind the front door and

then went to look for the invitation Jesse had given me the week before. The dress code was supposed to be casual, but I figured that casual according to the Lamberts was actually what I considered pretty fancy. Before showering I searched through my closet finding a slinky, off-the-shoulder top and a skirt that hit a few inches above my knees to pair it with.

Since I didn't feel like taking the train, I called a taxi. By the time I got to the Lamberts' fancy Manhattan apartment building, I was a mess of jittery nerves. I wasn't used to spending my time around people like them and worried that I'd do something to embarrass myself, like saying the wrong thing or breaking something obscenely expensive.

The elevator took me straight to the Lamberts' rooftop deck. After the doors opened I stepped out, admiring the amazing three-hundred-sixty-degree view of the city skyline. I spotted Jesse and Justin sitting beside each other on a patio sofa and walked over to say hello. Both of them got up to give me cheek kisses.

"Where's Greg?" Jesse asked.

"He decided he'd rather spend the day with a friend of his," I said, not even trying to hold in the resentment I still felt.

"You sound mad," Jesse replied. "Does he know that he pissed you off?"

"Yeah. We got into it this morning." I stopped myself from saying anything more because this was supposed to be Jesse's shower, and I was there to celebrate her upcoming wedding, not talk about my issues. I scanned the crowd to see if I recognized anyone. Jesse's brother, Mike, and his wife, Mel, were there. I gave them a quick wave.

"Do you want anything to eat or drink?" Justin asked. "We've got steaks and chicken grilling, and about five different kinds of salad. There's also a full bar."

The Lamberts didn't really seem like the beer-drinking type, so I asked for a rum and Coke and whatever was ready from the grill.

"Okay, I'll be right back." Justin headed toward a long table covered in white linen and set up with plates, silverware, and napkins.

"You look nice," Jesse said as I sat down beside her.

"Thanks," I replied, even though I'd just begun to notice that my outfit had a lot less fabric than just about everyone else's. I tugged at my shirt, trying to cover up as much as I could. "Maybe I should've worn a jacket."

"No. You look amazing." Jesse smiled and took a sip of her drink. "And I'm not the only one that thinks so."

I furrowed my brows. "What are you talking about?"

"You might not have noticed, but Justin's brother, Jeff, has been staring at you since you got off the elevator."

I craned my neck to see if I could find him and spotted him standing next to the grill with his dad and younger brother, James. I love a tall man, and Jeff was the tallest of the three Lambert boys. He had to be at least six feet.

"Good Lord, he's hot," I said, prompting a smile from Jesse.

Jeff's wavy hair was sandy brown, and though he was standing too far for me to get a good look, I remembered noticing how beautiful his blue eyes were when we'd first met and the way they reminded me of a perfectly cloudless sky on a sunny day. I didn't know Jeff well, but I could tell he was the kind of man smart women stayed away from. A man that was too pretty for anyone's good. Before Greg, I'd dated too many guys like that. Still, it didn't hurt to admire his assets from afar—until he noticed me checking him out.

His smile made me realize he'd caught me staring. Too late, I looked away. I'd been at Jesse's party for all of ten minutes and had already managed to embarrass myself.

As Jeff approached, I replayed the same mantra in my head over and over. *You're engaged, you're engaged.*

"It's nice to see you again." He grinned at me like he was some sort of mind reader and had pulled all the little dirty thoughts I'd had of him right out of my head. "Susan, right?"

"You remembered," I said, pretending to sound impressed.

"You're not easy to forget," he replied with a wink.

I looked around for the girl who had been with him the last time we'd met. With her model-good looks she wasn't the type of woman to blend into a crowd. I was about to ask Jeff why his girlfriend hadn't made it to the party when Justin walked up with a plate of potato salad and grilled chicken in one hand and a drink in the other.

"Is my brother flirting?" he asked, reaching down to put the plate and my drink on a side table. "He has a nasty habit of doing that."

"Hey," Jeff said, giving his brother a playful push. "I don't go around messing up your mojo."

"Mojo?" I said, trying not to laugh. "Is that what it's called?"

"Sorry to burst your bubble, Jeff," Jesse said. "You can use all the mojo you've got, but it's wasted on Susan. She's engaged."

I was almost disappointed by Jesse's announcement. It wasn't as if I could keep my engagement a secret, what with the ring I had on my finger and all, but I'd enjoyed pretending for a moment that someone as gorgeous as Jeff actually found me attractive enough to flirt with. Not that I didn't see myself as good-looking, but I knew for a fact that I was eight years older than Jeff. Although I doubted he was aware of our age difference. Luckily for me, most people told me I looked younger than I was. Cute was what I was often called, a word I'd come to realize that people liked to use when describing petite girls like me. I had just gotten my long, dark brown, wavy hair cut so that it fell a few inches down my back, and had a few highlights put in to bring out the hazel in my eyes. My new look, along with the outfit I'd chosen, was probably what had Jeff acting so friendly.

"Just my luck. Why are all the good ones always taken?"

"Mom's got a few eligible ladies lined up for you," Justin said. "All you need to do is say the word."

Jeff shook his head. "No, thank you."

Jesse smirked. "I still can't get over how different you and Justin are from the rest of your family."

"Yeah. It sucks for Mom that she got stuck with two black sheep instead of one," Jeff said.

Most of what I knew about Mr. and Mrs. Lambert came from Jesse. They were both successful investment bankers and, as a result, fabulously wealthy. Mrs. Lambert was adamantly opposed to Justin's choice of girlfriend when he and Jesse first got together, partly because she thought Jesse was after Justin's money. She was overprotective of him, not just because he was her firstborn, but because he'd almost died during a tour of duty in Afghanistan. Instead of losing his life, he'd lost both his legs and now had prosthetic ones. Mrs. Lambert just didn't believe that Jesse could truly love her son, given all the issues he had. Jesse was convinced that Mrs. Lambert wanted to keep Justin all to herself, that she wanted him to be the one child of hers who never left home and always depended on his mama for everything. It had taken a lot for Allison to finally accept that Justin and Jesse were meant for each other.

Jesse was madly, deeply in love with her fiancé, and had been since the two of them started working together at a community center in the Upper West Side a few summers ago. She didn't want to admit it at first, but I saw it all over her face every time she had mentioned his name.

I wondered if Mrs. Lambert would be as possessive of her middle child. Jeff didn't have the same medical issues Justin did, and I remembered Jesse telling me that Jeff had followed the path his parents wanted him to, going to college instead of joining the Navy. Perhaps that was enough for the ultimate helicopter mom to back off and let her son decide whom he should date.

Not that it was any business of mine. Even if Jeff and I were interested in each other, which of course we weren't, I was engaged.

I vowed to stop letting my mind wander to places I knew it shouldn't and excused myself to say hi to and make small talk with a few other people I knew from school before finally working up the courage to make my way over to Justin's parents. My mother had never trusted or particularly liked rich city people, and had instilled that same distrust in me. But it would be rude for me not to greet my best friend's future in-laws. Despite my nerves, I managed an awkward hello.

"Susan, right?" Mrs. Lambert said. "You're Jesse's maid of honor?" It surprised me that she actually remembered my name.

"Yup, that's me," I replied, somehow managing a smile.

She put her hand on my arm. "I appreciate you letting me throw this wedding shower, even though I know technically it's the bridesmaid's job."

"Oh, yeah, well. It's what Jesse wanted," I said.

"Are you enjoying yourself?"

"Yes. Your deck here is amazing, and the food, too." I was impressed by the mix of formal and casual. They'd hired a bartender, and the linens and tableware were clearly top of the line, but the food, even though it was most likely catered, wasn't super fancy, and there were no waiters with bowties handing out hors d'oeuvres and champagne.

"Then, please, feel free to help yourself to more," Mrs. Lambert said, sounding rather disinterested. I got the feeling that she had better things to do than have a conversation with me so I excused myself, and went to look for Jesse again.

When I found her, she was sitting by herself, which gave me a chance to ask her the question that had been on my mind since I first spotted her fiancé's brother. "So, how come Jeff's girlfriend isn't here?"

Jesse made a strange face and looked over her shoulder. "They broke up a few weeks ago," she whispered. "And it was *ugly*. He's basically decided he's done with relationships. I don't think he's taken the same girl out more than once since the break-up. "

I wanted to ask her for details, but spotted Jeff and Justin walking toward us with platefuls of cake in their hands. They handed us each a slice.

"Thank you," I said, giving Jeff a shy smile. I lifted a forkful of cake into my mouth. Despite how delicious it was, the way Jeff was looking at me made me too nervous to eat. I put my plate down on the table and clasped my hands together in front of me trying to think of something clever to say. Before I could, Jesse and Justin excused themselves to go and mingle with their other guests, leaving me alone with Jeff.

Jeff reached for my left hand, grasping me by my fingers. "So," he said, looking down at my ring, "you really are engaged."

"You say that like you're surprised." I'd already had one rum and Coke and a glass of champagne and was tipsy enough that I didn't have as tight a reign on my words as I normally did. "Is it that hard to believe someone would want to marry me?"

"No! A gorgeous girl like you. Of course that's not what I'm saying." Jeff let go of my hand. "I just don't know why anybody would want to get hitched to one person for the rest of their life. It's crazy."

"Oh, so you're one of those?"

"One of what?"

"Those guys that go around saying 'there are too many fish in the sea,' or 'why buy the cow when you can get the milk for free?'"

Jeff laughed, but didn't attempt a denial. "Well, not all of us are as lucky as Justin and Jesse. Most people don't wind up finding true love."

"So you do at least believe it exists?"

"What? True love?" he said. "I used to, but I'm not so sure anymore. To be honest, if it wasn't for my brother and his fiancée, I'd say the whole thing was a myth."

"Well, I believe in it."

"I should hope so, you are engaged, after all."

Jeff's brother, James, called him over and he excused himself before I had a chance to reply. Not that I even knew what to say. Yeah, I was engaged, but to my true love? A sinking feeling came over me. Even though Greg and I loved each other, something was missing.

I took a few more bites of cake before deciding that I needed another drink. But even that didn't settle the hollow feeling that had begun to settle somewhere in my gut. Trying to ignore it, I found Justin's parents and thanked them again. Then I said my goodbyes to Jesse and told her I'd see her on Friday at her wedding rehearsal.

On my way to the elevator I heard my name being called. Before I had a chance to turn my head, I felt a hand on my shoulder.

"It was nice seeing you again, Susan," Jeff said. The sun had just started to go down, casting a colorful glow on the horizon that reflected in his eyes. How was it that he looked even more gorgeous today than he had a few months ago, when we'd first met? Maybe the girl draped over his arm last time had something to do with it. "We should get together, the four of us—you and me, Justin and Jesse—at least once before you get married."

My face heated at his suggestion. *Why before I got married?* "We will be, next week." I kept my voice light. Perhaps I was reading more into Jeff's invitation than I needed to.

"What do you mean?"

"I'm Jesse's maid of honor, and you're Justin's best man. That means we'll see each other on Friday at the rehearsal."

"That's not exactly what I had in mind. I was thinking more along the lines of catching a movie or going out for drinks," he said with a flirtatious smile. "As friends, of course, unless you change your mind about this whole 'getting married' thing."

Once again, I felt my face flame. "Did you tease your brother like this after he and Jesse got engaged?" I asked, doing my best to hide how flustered he was making me feel.

Jeff's expression grew serious. "It's like I said. Those two are different. They were meant to be together."

I couldn't argue that. Jesse and Justin had been through their share of ups and downs. Mostly because of Mrs. Lambert. She was partly to blame for the two of them breaking up a little over a year ago. I'd never seen Jesse more devastated than when her relationship with Justin ended. Thankfully, they were able to find their way back to each other. And even though it had taken time, Jesse and her soon-to-be mother-in-law, had forged a good relationship, despite the fact that they couldn't be two more different people. Justin's parents were very well off, and he came from a true all-American family, while Jesse was the daughter of Croatian immigrants who knew what it meant to struggle.

"And you don't think there's someone out there you were meant to be with?"

"I should be asking you that, since you're the one who's engaged," Jeff said. "Are you sure what's-his-name is really the one for you?"

"His name is Greg. And yes, he's the one for me," I replied, hoping that my tone of voice didn't betray my true feelings. How had we stumbled onto this topic of conversation again?

"Well, then I'm happy for you."

I managed a smile despite the jittery way Jeff made me feel. He was standing close enough to me that I could feel the heat from his body and smell the spicy scent of his cologne.

"It's late," I said. "I should get going. It was nice seeing you again."

"Yes, it was," he agreed.

I managed to make it to the elevator without tripping over my feet.

On the train ride back to Brooklyn I replayed my conversation with Jeff in my mind, questioning if anything he'd said to me had been more than just flirtatious banter. I couldn't help but wonder what would've happened if I'd given him any indication that I was interested. Would he have tried to talk me into going out with him? Or was he after something else? He'd all but told me straight out he wasn't a one-woman type of guy, which meant that he wasn't looking for anything serious. A disappointing, but not surprising, thought. But I would've sworn that the last time I'd seen him, when he was with his now ex-girlfriend, he seemed completely devoted to her. I made a mental note to ask Jesse about it the next time I saw her.

After arriving home, Bailey greeted me like he always did. I gave him a little scratch under his chin before realizing that something seemed strange. I was used to coming home to lights on and the sound of the TV, but instead the apartment was eerily silent and dark. I flicked the light on in the living room, surprised that Greg wasn't home yet. I sat down on the couch, happy that for once the remote control was mine. After flipping through every channel twice and finding nothing I wanted to watch, I decided I'd rather crawl under my covers with a good book.

As I headed to my bedroom, I noticed a piece of paper taped to the door with my name on it, written in Greg's sloppy cursive. Afraid, I stared at it, knowing somehow that I wasn't going to like whatever was written on it.

Chapter 3
The Note

I unfolded the paper and began to read.

Sue,

    I think we've both known for some time that things between us aren't working anymore. It's time one of us finally did something about it. While you were at Jesse's party I moved my stuff out. It's easier this way. I want us to go our separate ways without fighting.

    We've been together a long time, so I didn't want to admit the truth. We're just not meant for each other. I wish you nothing but the best and hope one day we can at least be friends.

    Greg

What the holy hell?! I read Greg's letter over two more times before his words truly sank in. Then I pushed open the bedroom door and took a look around the room. Everything seemed the same. Not that it wouldn't. Greg didn't have any knick-knacks. His belongings would be inside the dresser, not on top of it. I pulled open the drawers and found them all empty—not a single shirt or pair of underwear remained. I ran into the bathroom next and opened the medicine cabinet. His toothbrush was gone, along with his cologne, razor, and deodorant.

I stood in front of the cabinet, staring at its contents with my mouth open. Who did this kind of shit? What kind of person moved out of the apartment he shared with his fiancée, leaving only a letter behind? I knew things weren't perfect between us, but we'd just had sex less than twelve hours ago. I should have been suspicious then; Greg didn't typically take his time the way he had this morning, or rested with me in his arms afterward. Apparently he'd wanted to savor our last time. One final fuck before he moved on with his life. Stunned, I made my way back into the living room and fell onto the couch, not sure what to think, much less do. While I'd been trying to come up with ways to save our relationship, he'd been planning on leaving it without so much as a word of warning. I just sat there for a few minutes while everything sank in. My emotions shifted suddenly. I went from being shocked to being angry. No, not angry. Fuming. I picked up my cell phone and dialed Greg's number, ready to give him a piece of my mind. This was not how you ended a relationship.

He didn't answer his phone. I tried again after a few minutes, but the call went to voicemail again.

"You son of a bitch!" I yelled, unleashing my fury on his answering machine. "I can't believe you didn't have the balls to tell me to my face that you wanted to break up."

Every few minutes I alternated between feeling intensely angry and wanting to cry. I knew Greg and I had problems, but we were engaged and we'd been living together for years. He owed me more than a note taped to my door.

I finally broke down. Tears fell from my eyes as I curled myself into a ball on the couch. Problems or not, I was used to having Greg around, how was I supposed to face waking up every morning to an empty apartment?

My phone rang. Certain that it was Greg calling me back I picked it up without even bothering to check caller ID first. I launched into a tirade. "You rotten, stinking piece of shit…," I began.

"Susan?" It was Jesse.

I had no choice but to tell her what had happened, even though I didn't feel like talking about it. I knew Jesse well enough to realize that she wouldn't let it go until I told her what had me so upset.

I tried to form words but all that came out were more tears and that awful sobbing noise that accompanies them.

"You're starting to scare me, Sue," Jesse finally said.

Crying wasn't something I did very often. In fact, it wasn't something I remembered ever doing in front of Jesse. She was usually the one who came to me needing a shoulder to cry on, not the other way around. I'd never really had any reason to before. "Greg and I broke up," I finally managed to tell her.

"What? When did this happen? You were just here like an hour ago."

"Apparently your wedding shower gave him the perfect opportunity to pack his shit behind my back and leave me a dumb-ass note. That's why he didn't want to come with me to your shower. He's probably been planning this all week."

"He moved out?" Jesse said, her voice full of the same disbelief I felt.

I read Greg's note to her and told her about searching through his drawers, only to find them empty.

"Son of a bitch," Jesse said. "I can't believe he'd do that to you. If I *ever* see him again I'm going to punch him in the face."

"Not if I get to him first."

"I'm calling a cab and coming over. I'll be there in half an hour, okay?"

"Jesse, you don't have to do that. You and Justin just had your wedding shower. You should be with him."

"He'll understand. Besides, we were together all afternoon," she said, "and you shouldn't be alone right now."

I felt like I should argue with her and insist that I didn't need her to come over, but truthfully, she was right. I didn't want to be alone.

I got up and went to the fridge to look for a beer while I waited for Jesse to arrive. Every single bottle was gone. Greg must have taken them with him. I slammed the refrigerator shut, pissed that he couldn't be bothered to at least leave me one beer when I needed it the most. I was tempted to run downstairs and into the bar that I literally lived right over, but I was friendly with the bartenders who worked there, which meant they'd probably ask what had upset me. I wasn't in the mood to broadcast the news just yet.

Instead I walked a few blocks over to one of the neighborhood bodegas that stayed open all night, and bought a six-pack. I was almost done with my fourth beer by the time Jesse arrived. With my head spinning from too much alcohol, I only vaguely remembered her finding me on the couch and helping me to my bedroom, but everything after that was foggy.

I woke up the next morning with a raging headache and found that Jesse had spent the night. She tried just about every hangover treatment known to man before I told her to stop bothering. Ibuprofen took the edge off, and the eggs and coffee she made for breakfast helped a little, too.

She reached for my hand across the table, and I couldn't help but notice that my ring was still on. If I hocked it, maybe I'd get enough money to cover Greg's share of the rent until I found a roommate.

"Listen, Susan," she said. "I was thinking that if you want to change your mind about being my maid of honor, I'd totally understand."

"What? No. Why would I do that?" I asked, surprised by her suggestion. Despite the fact that my relationship had just imploded, there was no way I was going to bail on my best friend. "Of course I still want to be your maid of honor."

"You've got a lot going on, and my wedding is going to be small. The planner Allison hired pretty much has everything under control. I don't really have to have a maid of honor."

"Yes, you do," I insisted. No matter how crummy I felt, I wasn't about to let her down. "Although I hate to tell you this, I'm pretty sure you'll be down one groomsman."

"I don't care about that. Greg can go fuck himself after what he did to you."

I shook my head. "I still can't believe he's gone."

"How did this happen? Were you guys arguing about stuff?"

"No, not really. At least not recently. But things haven't been the same between us for a while." I sighed. "Ever since he lost his job a few months ago, things changed. We went from arguing all the time to barely talking to each other. I kept telling myself it was just a phase, that eventually we'd reconnect, but I don't think either of us really knew how to make that happen."

"So that's why you guys never set a date for your wedding."

"Not everyone can be like you and Justin," I said. It wasn't until the words were out that I realized how petty and jealous I sounded. I was doing a terrible job of keeping my green-eyed monster in check. But it was hard not to feel envious. Justin had proposed to Jesse only a few months ago, and in less than a week they were going to be married. Greg and I had been engaged for almost two years and we were never going to make it to the altar.

Jesse didn't seem to take offense. I figured she knew how I was feeling. It wasn't that long ago that our situations had been reversed. I'd just gotten engaged to Greg, just as she was going through a rough patch with Justin. "How come you never told me that you and Greg were having problems?"

I shrugged. "I guess I didn't want to admit it to myself."

"Oh, Susan." Jesse got up from the table, came around to my side and wrapped her arms around me. "I'm so sorry."

"So am I." Although I wasn't really sure what I was sorrier about—that my relationship was over, that Greg had left with rent due in another week, or that I'd wasted so many months with him instead of moving on sooner.

"Where do you suppose he went?"

I thought about it. "I don't know. His mom's house, maybe? Although I think she'd have called me if she knew Greg was planning to break up with me." I'd become close with Greg's family, especially his mother.

"You know what? We need to do something fun today. Something that will take your mind off Greg. I say we get dressed, go see a movie, and stuff our faces with popcorn and candy."

"I'm not sure I can sit through a whole movie," I said. "Besides, don't you have like a million wedding things to do?"

"Not really."

I wanted to hug her. It was less than a week before her wedding, but instead of freaking out and acting like a bridezilla, she was making time for me. "I need to take Bailey out. Do you want to come along?"

She smiled. "Sure. Sounds like fun, actually."

Jesse hung out with me for another few hours. After walking Bailey, we stuffed our faces with greasy pizza. After, I managed to convince her that I was fine and didn't need her to stay. Reluctantly, she said good-bye even though it was obvious she was worried about leaving me alone. I adored her for being such a good friend.

As soon as she left I tried calling Greg again. This time he answered. Or at least I thought it was him until I heard a woman's voice on the line.

Before I had a chance to utter a single word she said, "Look, I get it, you're pissed because Greg dumped you, but when a guy doesn't answer your calls it means *stop calling.*"

Who was this strange woman telling me to stop calling the man who up until yesterday had been my fiancé? I wanted to keep my cool, but there was just no way that was happening.

"Who is this?" I demanded.

"Greg's girlfriend."

"His what?!" For a moment I almost thought I was being pranked. This could not be happening.

"You heard me."

I wanted to know exactly how long Greg had been cheating on me, but I got the feeling this new girlfriend of his wasn't going to give me any answers. She must've been the reason Greg had supposedly been spending so much time at work. For a moment I was tempted to ask her if she knew her boyfriend had gotten in one last fuck with me before leaving our bed for hers, but I decided not to bother. The two of them could have each other. I hung up without saying another word and just sat there wondering how I'd been so blind and stupid. The Greg I'd gotten engaged to almost two years ago wouldn't have hurt me this way. How was it possible that someone could change so drastically?

Chapter 4
A Rehearsal and a Wedding

Falling asleep in an empty bed turned out to be harder than I thought it would be. Bailey must've sensed that Greg was gone and how alone that left me feeling, because not long after I pulled the covers over my body he curled up next to me. I forgot how nice it was to sleep with him snuggled beside me.

In the morning I found myself grateful for the first time since graduation that I didn't have a job to go to. There was simply no way I could function properly in the state I was in. I drowned my sorrows in ice cream and cookies and spent most of my time on the couch mindlessly watching home improvement shows. Jesse checked up on me often. Every time she did, I tried convincing her and myself that the hurt had begun to ease up.

To my utter astonishment, that eventually turned out to be true. I thought about Greg a little bit less every day and by the end of the week I was confident that I could make it through Jesse's rehearsal and dinner without a meltdown.

Jesse and Justin's wedding was going to be held at one of the most gorgeous places in all of New York—the Brooklyn Botanical Garden. I had no idea how they even managed to book a wedding there on such short notice, but I supposed Lambert money probably had a hand in that.

Jesse's wedding planner had us walk through the processional and recessional a few times before she was satisfied that the wedding would go off without a hitch. That meant quite a bit of walking arm in arm with Jeff, since he was the best man. I tried my best to avoid eye contact with him because those luscious blue eyes of his seemed to be drinking me in with every glance. And that smile of his, full of mischief. I alternated between lust for him and hatred for the male sex in general. My frustrating mix of emotions made me almost regret not taking Jesse up on her offer to let me out of my maid of honor duties. I kept telling myself over and over *I can do this. I can do this.*

Afterward, Justin's parents ushered us all into taxis that drove us to a restaurant in Brooklyn Heights for dinner. As if the rehearsal hadn't been torturous enough, Jeff and I got seated beside each other. I was half-tempted to lean over and whisper into his ear that I'd be his later if he wanted. Maybe sex with a hotter-than-hot guy would help me get over the bitterness Greg had left with me with. But I wasn't a one-night stand kind of girl, and I didn't think my already damaged pride could take spending the night with someone who I'd probably never hear from again.

"You're awfully quiet today," Jeff said after the waitress left with everyone's orders.

"That's what happens when your fiancé dumps you less than a week before your best friend's wedding," I said, shocked at myself for the way I'd just blurted those words out. I took a sip of wine, even though I wanted to gulp down the whole glassful.

Too bad your best friend's rehearsal dinner was hardly the ideal place to get drunk.

Jeff looked at me like I'd just told him aliens had invaded Earth. "You and your fiancé broke up?"

"Yup," I said, taking another sip of wine and praying that tears wouldn't start rolling down my face. I really thought I'd moved beyond crying over Greg. Apparently I was wrong.

"Sheesh. I'm sorry to hear that."

"Really? Weren't you just telling me that you didn't understand why anyone would want to spend the rest of their life with just one person?"

"Yeah, but…"

"I guess you were right, because clearly Greg didn't want to. I was just too stupid to see it. And apparently he's already found himself another fish," I said, grateful that it was noisy enough in the restaurant that only Jeff could hear me.

He rested his hand on top of mine. "Susan, I'm sorry. A guy like that . . ." He shook his head. "He doesn't deserve you. It's his loss."

I knew he was only trying to be nice, but somehow I'd jumped aboard the negative train and had no plans to get off. "No, not really, considering he used to pay half the rent. Now I'm going to have to find a roommate to come up with his share," I said, bitterly. "Maybe you'd like to move in and get a taste for how real people live."

Jeff looked at me with a blank expression on his face. Perhaps I'd gone too far. What happened between me and Greg wasn't his fault, yet here I was lashing out at him. I pulled my hand away from his. "Excuse me. I need to go to the bathroom," I said, before rushing off in search of the restroom, where I locked myself inside of one of the stalls and started to cry.

A minute later I heard Jesse calling my name. She knocked on the door of the stall. "Open up," she said.

I threw the latch back. Jesse walked in and wrapped her arms around me. "He's not worth your tears," she said.

"I know. I know," I said, sobbing on her shoulder. "It's just that I'm so angry."

"He wasn't the person you thought he was. It's a lot better that you found out now."

That was certainly true. "I don't even think I'm crying about him in particular. It's getting past the dream I had in my head of the two of us happily married that's so hard. Even though we were having problems, a part of me still believed he'd go back to being the Greg I fell in love with, and everything would work out," I explained. "Instead, I'm probably going to be alone for the rest of my life . . ."

"What are you talking about? People break up all the time; it doesn't mean you'll be alone. There are plenty of guys who would love to have a chance with you."

"And you know this how?"

Jesse grasped my hand and pulled me out of the bathroom stall and over to the mirror. She pointed to my reflection. "That's how I know. Because even with your eyes all red and puffy you're still beautiful. And not only are you beautiful, but you're funny and kind, and you mix a mean cocktail."

I started to laugh so hard that more tears fell. Jesse gave me another hug. "I feel like I'm ruining your rehearsal dinner."

"Oh, come on, Sue. Of course you're not. Besides, you know

I'd rather hang out with you in here than sit through a stuffy dinner with Justin's family."

I knew she was just being nice, and I loved her for it. Because even though Justin's family could be a little on the stuffy side, Jesse adored them anyway. I took a deep breath and rinsed my face. "We should go back."

"Are you sure you're going to be all right?"

I nodded as Jesse reached for my hand. She led me back to our table.

"You okay?" Jeff asked after I sat back down next to him.

"I'm assuming you were the one who sent Jesse after me?"

"It seemed like the right thing to do," Jeff said, sounding worried that maybe it hadn't been.

"It was." I managed a weak smile. "Thank you."

He took a piece of paper out of his pocket and scribbled something down on it. "My number, in case you want to talk."

I smirked. "Just talk?"

"Believe it or not, I can be a decent guy sometimes, and a good friend. Of course if you want more, I certainly wouldn't say no," he said with that mischievous grin of his that made me melt a little inside even though I knew I shouldn't let him do that to me.

Jeff's flirting was just the ego boost I needed, and by the time dessert came around, Greg, and the way he dumped me, had been pushed to the back of my mind. After I finished my meal I made sure to graciously thank Justin's parents before giving Jesse a hug. I reached for my jacket from the back of my chair, but Jeff grabbed it before I could.

"Let me help you," he said, standing and holding it out for

me so that I could put my arms through the sleeves.

"Such a gentleman," I quipped.

"Just trying to show you that I'm not always a jerk," he said as I lifted the strap of my purse onto my shoulder.

I turned around to face him. "You weren't being a jerk. I was."

"Seriously, Susan. I'm sorry about what happened."

"Forget about it," I said. "Maybe you're right. Marriage isn't for everybody."

Instead of heading home I took a walk down to the promenade where the view of the city was beautiful, especially at night with the Manhattan skyline lit up. I loved the lights, especially those of the Empire State Building. But Brooklyn Promenade was also one of those places that attracted couples who enjoyed strolling along the cobbled walkway, stopping every few minutes to take selfies and share kisses.

Since there was only so much of that I could take, I turned around and made my way to the train station. Just as I got back to my apartment my phone dinged with a text from Greg.

Wondering if we can meet sometime so I can get the ring back.

I read his message again, trying to wrap my mind around the nerve it took to send me that text. He really was a son of a bitch—and never ever going to get the engagement ring he'd given me back.

So sorry, but I don't have it anymore.

He texted me back. *What do you mean you don't have it anymore????*

Had to sell it to pay your half of the damn rent.

He apparently had nothing to say after that. I wondered if he planned on giving the ring to his new girl or if he just wanted to see how much he could get for it. Not that it mattered. I still had the ring, but I wasn't about to tell him that. Especially because now that he'd asked for it back, I was more determined than ever to take it to a pawn shop.

I went to bed fuming and by morning I was still angry. But I had maid of honor duties to fulfill so I did what I always did when I needed to blow off some steam and took Bailey for a run. The mixture of exercise endorphins and play time with Bailey helped push Greg out of my head.

A few hours later when the limo arrived to pick me up and take me to the Brooklyn Botanical Garden I ran down the stairs brimming with excitement. I was the last of the bridal party to arrive. Mel and Sophia were getting makeup and hair done by professional stylists. Jesse's was already finished, so I went over to help her into her dress while I waited for my turn with the stylist.

I greeted her with a hug. "I can't believe I'm actually getting married today," she said, sounding partly nervous and partly excited.

"You picked a real good guy, Jesse," I said, reaching for one of her shaking hands. "The two of you are going to be so happy together."

"I can't wait to see Justin." It looked like she was trying to hold back happy tears. "I'm used to him in track pants and T-shirts, not a tuxedo."

"Well then, we'd better get you into your dress." I reached for it and unzipped the back before sliding it off the hanger. The dress wasn't poufy or super ornate, and didn't have a long train, so she didn't really need much help. Jesse turned to look at herself in the mirror.

"You look amazing," I said. Her dark hair was partly pulled back and held in place with a floral tiara; the rest curled down her back in soft waves.

She waved to one of the stylists who'd just finished applying Mel's makeup. "This is my maid of honor," Jesse said to her.

"Nice to meet you." I shook her hand and she glanced down at her watch. "We better get going. The wedding is going to start soon."

While Jesse went to talk to Mel and Sophia my hair got pinned into a neat chignon. After the stylist applied my makeup I looked at my reflection, appreciating the way the green dress I wore along with the warm earth tones of my makeup brought out the hazel in my eyes.

Jesse walked over to me with a grin on her face and her cell phone in her hand. "Selfie time."

She snapped a few photos and then I took out my phone too. Jesse had a professional photographer who was bound to take a thousand pictures, but there was something intimate and personal about a selfie with your best friend that no one else could capture.

A few minutes later Mrs. Lambert knocked on the dressing room door. "Is everything on schedule?" she asked, poking her head inside.

Jesse turned to reply. "We're all ready."

Mrs. Lambert gaped at her before opening the door. "Oh, Jesse, you look absolutely stunning." She gave her soon to be daughter-in-law a hug. "I still can't believe Justin is getting married today. It feels like only yesterday I was changing his diapers."

Somehow I could not imagine Justin as a baby in diapers, or Mrs. Lambert changing them. Seconds after she'd left, Jesse's wedding planner knocked and called out, "The ceremony is going to start soon."

"We're ready," I told her.

With the help of the wedding planner, the other girls and I lined up in the right order. Since Jesse's parents weren't going to be coming to the wedding, Justin's parents were included in the processional instead, which meant Mrs. Lambert would be the first person to walk down the aisle. She gave Jesse a kiss on her cheek before leaving the rest of us to make last-minute adjustments to our hair and makeup. A few minutes later the wedding music began. I glanced at Jesse, who looked like she'd just jumped out of a page in a bridal magazine. By the way she was clutching her bouquet of orange and red calla lilies tightly in her hands I could tell she was nervous. I gave her a hug, and whispered in her ear, "Just breathe."

It must've been the right thing to say because it made her smile. Along with Mel and Sophia, the four of us headed toward the atrium where the wedding ceremony and reception would take place. While Mel and Sophia walked down the aisle I did a little last-minute primping of Jesse's hair, and then it was my turn to make my way toward the altar.

The atrium was gorgeously decorated. Bouquets of red and orange flowers provided a pop of color among all the white. But it was the floor to ceiling glass walls which afforded amazing views of the gardens outside that I found the most breathtaking.

I loved Jesse's style, simple and elegant, and a bit rustic at the same time. As I walked down the aisle I remembered the wedding planner's instructions about not holding my bouquet too high and I made sure to walk slowly and carefully so that I wouldn't trip in my high heels.

Jesse looked absolutely stunning as she took her turn down the aisle. Everyone's eyes were on her, but I couldn't help but watch Justin's face. It got brighter and brighter, his smile bigger and bigger with every step she took. It was beautiful to see. I truly had never met two more perfectly matched people than Jesse and Justin.

Chapter 5
The Reception

I wasn't one for crying in public, but I couldn't help but get teary-eyed as Jesse and Justin exchanged their vows. After they finished, the two of them kissed before the wedding officiant declared them husband and wife. Then the wedding recessional began. I looped my arm through Jeff's, trying to ignore the seductive smile he wore.

"You look beautiful," He whispered as he eyed me all the way from my strappy heels to my blushing face. I tried to ignore the fluttery feeling inside and reminded myself of what Jeff was. A player. He led me past the wedding guests and over to a small cocktail area set up for guests to congregate while the ceremony area got transformed for the reception.

Jeff looked movie-star handsome in his tuxedo. For a moment I wondered what kissing him would feel like. My face heated at the thought. Thankfully, once this night was over it would probably be a long time before I saw him again, since we'd only been thrown together over the past few weeks because of the wedding. If Jeff kept looking at me the way he was now, and kept saying the things I needed to hear, I didn't think I could continue fighting my desire. Not when I was still so raw over being dumped, and not when something told me he wanted me in his bed.

When the recessional was over a photographer ushered the bridal party outside to take pictures. She had all sorts of creative poses she wanted us to try, almost all of them requiring me to get close—very close—to Jeff. With each picture I became more and more convinced that the photographer was trying to drive me crazy.

After my presence in the photo shoot was no longer required, I made a beeline for the bar and ordered a cosmopolitan, while Jeff stayed behind for family pictures. I sat at the bar and took a few sips of my drink, trying to talk myself out of the crazy attraction I had for him, rationalizing that the only reason I was so enticed by him was because of how low Greg had left me feeling. But the more I tried telling myself to stop thinking about Jeff, the more I kept picturing that sexy smile of his.

I was so deep in thought I didn't notice as Jeff walked up behind me. "You don't strike me as a cosmo drinker," he said, startling me and causing me to practically spill my drink.

"Aren't you supposed to be taking pictures?" I said.

"That's all done, which means now it's time to dance," Jeff said, taking one of my hands in his.

"Slow down, party boy." I pulled my hand back and rested it on his chest. "We've got dinner, wedding toasts, and cake-cutting to get through first."

"Well, since I get the pleasure of sitting next to you, I think I can handle waiting."

"I don't think it works that way. Aren't you supposed to be

sitting next to the bride?" At least that's what Jesse had told me when she explained wedding party seating etiquette to me.

"It works that way when you ask your brother and his fiancée to switch things around for you."

"Big mistake," I said, trying for a little humor to ease the knots in my stomach. "By the end of the night you'll be sick of me."

He arched an eyebrow. "I can guarantee you that won't be the case."

An announcement that the reception area was ready interrupted our conversation. Jeff held his hand out and I took it. As we walked over to our table I marveled at how quickly and efficiently the staff had transformed the room. Tables had been set up, and wide, colorful ribbons had been tied around the backs of each chair. Sparkling chandeliers bathed the room in ambient light, making the space look almost as if it was glowing.

After the guests were all seated waiters came and went, filling glasses of wine and placing the first course down on the tables. I reached for my glass of merlot and took a sip just as Jeff leaned in close to me and whispered into my ear, "Did you know that it's tradition for the best man and maid of honor to hook up after the wedding?"

I almost choked. That was so not what I expected him to say. I glanced at him for a moment, not really knowing how to respond. Was I supposed to laugh, because clearly he was joking and didn't really think we were going to be having sex later?

"Why are you looking at me like that?" he said. "Already undressing me in your head, is that it?"

"Maybe just a little," I said, deciding to go along with it.

There was no me and Greg anymore, so I didn't see the harm in some innocent flirting.

"All I can say is that I'm pretty happy Jesse asked you to be her maid of honor instead of that girl," Jeff said, gesturing toward a friend of mine and Jesse's from college, Vivian, who was seated at the table next to ours.

"What's wrong with her? I think she's cute."

Jeff made a funny face. "She reminds me of my mom."

I burst out laughing. Vivian did kind of remind me of Mrs. Lambert with her obviously not natural blonde hair and too skinny frame.

"Are you always this funny, or is this comedy routine of yours just for my personal enjoyment?"

Jeff smiled. "You think I'm funny?"

He sounded surprised, and I couldn't help but wonder why. I supposed not everyone had the same sense of humor that Jeff did. I liked it, especially now. It was hard enough getting dumped the way I had, but watching your best friend get married to the man of her dreams less than a week after your own fiancé moved out wasn't easy. All this wedding stuff made it hard not to think about the fact that I was over thirty with absolutely no romantic prospects on the horizon. I'd always wanted to have children, and now I couldn't help but wonder if that was ever going to happen.

After most of the guests had finished their first course, Jeff stood up to toast Jesse and his brother. He spoke eloquently about true love and how he knew from the first time he saw Jesse and his brother together that the two of them were meant to be. For someone who made a point of letting it be known that he didn't believe in happily ever afters, his speech was not what I'd expected.

My toast followed his, and then it was Justin's parents' turn. Together they both officially welcomed Jesse into their family. I caught tears forming in the corner of Jesse's eyes and reached for her hand.

Dinner was served after, followed by the cutting of the cake, and then it was time for dancing. Jeff pulled me to the dance floor and rested his hands on my hips while the two of us swayed to the beat of the song that was playing. With every passing second, the room got warmer and warmer and I felt like I was melting in his arms. Jeff smelled like an intoxicating mixture of wine and expensive cologne.

"How are you doing?" he asked.

"I'm fine," I said, snapping back to reality. "Why wouldn't I be?"

"It can't be easy doing this whole wedding thing right after a break-up."

"I'm trying really hard not to think about that," I said, wishing he hadn't mentioned it.

"Sorry. Didn't mean to make you feel bad," he said. "It's just that I know how it feels to have to smile for everyone when it's the last thing you feel like doing."

He seemed really sincere. Which was no good. Not only was he handsome and funny, but he had a sensitive side, too. He was making it impossible for me not to be attracted to him.

"I still can't believe Greg just up and moved out of our apartment while I was at Jesse's wedding shower, and that he didn't have the guts to tell me he'd found someone else. The whole thing makes me feel so stupid." I hadn't intended to open up like that. As the words left my mouth, I wished I could take them back. Jeff wasn't interested in my problems. He was obviously the type of guy who was all about having fun and living in the moment, which meant he probably had zero interest in listening to my pathetic problems.

"You're not stupid, just naïve, like I used to be. It sucks thinking you've fallen in love and found the person you want to spend your life with, only to realize that you were totally wrong." I looked into his eyes as he spoke, trying to read him. "What's the point in going through that?" he continued, his voice hollow. "I don't get why people make promises they won't be able to keep. It makes no sense."

"Um, I get the feeling we aren't talking about me anymore."

Jeff hesitated for a moment. "Yes, we are. Greg wanted to marry you; that's what you thought would happen when he put that ring on your finger. But somewhere along the line he changed his mind and didn't even bother to clue you in."

I could tell he was trying to cover. "You're supposed to be cheering me up, not reminding me of my disastrous love life," I said, hoping my attempt at humor would bring the smile back to his face. Apparently Jesse hadn't been kidding when she said Jeff's recent break-up had been ugly.

Jeff leaned in closer and whispered seductively in my ear, "I can make you forget." His breath on my neck gave me goosebumps.

I stared into his eyes. My heart pounded and I so badly wanted to just say yes. A one-night stand wasn't something I'd ever done before, but why the hell not? It had only been a week since Greg left, but he'd already moved on with some other girl, so why shouldn't I move on with pretty much the most attractive man I'd ever laid eyes on? If casual sex had helped Jeff get over his recent break-up, maybe it would help me get over mine.

"What I want," I said, taking a step back from him before I found myself planting a kiss on those dreamy lips of his, "is another drink."

He grabbed my wrist. "I don't know if that's such a good idea, Susan. How many have you had so far?"

"Not enough," I said, before pulling my wrist free and heading over to the bar. Jeff followed me, but didn't say anything as I ordered a cosmo and finished it. Just as I was about to dive into another one, he wrested the glass from my hand.

"I know how you're feeling, but you don't need alcohol to forget about your broken heart. I have a much better way," he said. The tone of his voice matched the serious expression on his face. "But not if you're drunk. I'm not the kind of guy who takes advantage of someone who's had too much to drink."

"Well, aren't you the gentleman?"

"Sometimes," he replied in a husky voice.

"So what exactly are you proposing?" I said. "That we go to your place for a wild night of rebound sex?"

"Give me one good reason why we shouldn't." Jeff inched closer to me. He took hold of my chin, forcing me to meet his gaze. Good God, the man was handsome and funny, confident and strong, and he made me feel sexy. The next thing I knew he was kissing me and it felt good, damn good. Except we were at a wedding reception and there were tons of people all around us. People whom both of us knew. People that would be asking me what the hell I was thinking, making out with the groom's brother at my best friend's wedding. I pulled away.

"Not here."

Jeff smiled, reading into my words exactly what I wanted him to. "I just wanted to give you a little preview," he said.

Right. If that was the preview I couldn't wait for the main act.

Chapter 6
One Night Stand

No matter how badly I wanted to, as maid of honor, I couldn't just sneak out without a word. I craned my neck, looking for Jesse. She was in the middle of a dance with her father-in-law. I didn't want to interrupt the two of them, so instead I found Mel. When I told her I needed to leave early, she thankfully didn't ask why, and, even better, offered to help out, telling me that if Jesse needed anything she'd fill in for me.

Jeff and I managed to sneak out of the reception area without anyone noticing. We got into a waiting taxi. As soon as Jeff closed the door of the cab, he pulled me closer, pressing his lips on mine. Even though his kisses left me practically breathless, I was half-tempted to pull away and ask him what the hell we were doing, but I pushed those thoughts away, refusing to let myself overthink things. I just wanted to feel good again, to feel desired and sexy—something Jeff was insanely good at making happen. So why mess that up with questions I already knew the answers to?

When we got to Jeff's apartment building, he paid the taxi fare, took my hand, and helped me out of the cab. We walked inside his building and then onto the elevator. My heart hammered harder and harder with every floor we passed. By the time the elevator dinged and the door opened, I felt almost faint with anticipation.

I followed Jeff inside his apartment. "Wow. You've got a nice place." Admiring his décor temporarily took my mind off of what we were about to do. It felt like I'd just walked into a showroom at a Scandinavian furniture store. Everything was sleek, modern and obviously high-end, from the appliances in his kitchen to the TV that looked bigger than my kitchen table hanging above the fireplace. "I'm impressed."

"Don't be. My parents' money helped put me through an Ivy League university, and their connections got me the job I have now. I wouldn't have any of this if it wasn't for them," he explained, sounding almost apologetic. For some reason I admired his humility.

As I looked around, I couldn't help but wonder how many other women he'd brought here. Not my problem, I told myself. Jeff hadn't promised me anything other than a night to help me forget the shitty way Greg had left me feeling. And right now I was totally okay with that.

"Take a seat," he said, gesturing toward the couch.

After I did, he joined me. Being in the privacy of his apartment, with him so close beside me, made me nervous. I wasn't sure what I was supposed to be doing. Making small talk? Suggesting we watch TV? Or were we supposed to dive right in? I decided to choose the latter. Before Jeff had a chance to say or do anything I reached for him, kissing his lips and twining my fingers through his hair.

He was incredibly sexy and an amazing kisser. Everything about him seemed just right. He was eager without being forceful or rough. Eventually his lips made their way to my neck. As his tongue teased me, my body responded. I shuddered in his arms and moaned at the pleasure his kisses were giving me.

He began to take the pins out of my hair. "Jesus Christ. How many of these things did you use?" he said.

"Don't worry about my hair. Just leave it," I said, eager to get back to where we'd left off.

"No chance of that," Jeff replied, still fumbling with the hairpins. "You have the most gorgeous hair and I've been fantasizing about running my fingers through it ever since Justin and Jesse's party."

I certainly didn't want to deprive him of his fantasy, so I reached back to help him with the last few bobby pins.

"Your hair is so soft," Jeff moaned as his fingers combed through my hair. "Just like the rest of you."

His hands seemed to be everywhere. One minute he was running them through my hair, the next he was pulling the strap of my dress down to kiss my shoulder. His lips moved lower, grazing the skin along the neckline of my dress.

I managed to get his tie off and dropped it on the floor. I pulled his shirt free from his pants and reached under it. He unzipped my dress and both straps fell to the side. I had on a lacy black bra that clearly impressed him. He just stared at me for a moment before pressing his lips on mine again. As he fiddled with the clasp on the back of my bra I began to unbutton his shirt. Once that was off, along with my bra, Jeff leaned into me and I fell back onto the sofa with him on top of me. He kissed me and cupped one of my breasts with his hand, then he did the same to the other.

"Are you sure you want to do this?" he asked.

It was far too late for me to back out now. Fire ran through my veins. Jeff had me so turned on that there was no way I could hit the stop button. "Yes. I'm sure."

"Good," he breathed. "Because holy hell, I'm hard as a rock."

He took my hand and moved it across the bulge in his pants. Not like he really needed to do that. I could feel his desire when his body pressed into mine. He lifted me into his arms and carried me into his bedroom, laying me down on his king size bed. I squirmed out of my dress while Jeff unzipped his pants. He reached for my breasts again, cupping them with his hands before pressing his lips to my skin, then tasting me with his tongue. He teased my nipples with his mouth, causing me to writhe in pleasure. When his hand reached between my legs, I gasped.

He let out a soft moan when he realized that I was just as ready for him as he was for me.

"Can I kiss you down there?" he whispered into my ear.

My heart pounded as I murmured a yes. Greg hadn't done that to me in ages and I ached to experience that kind of pleasure again. As Jeff's tongue worked its magic I wanted to cry out. I felt my body shudder as he brought me to climax. A moment later he reached for the nightstand, fumbling with the drawer, and eventually pulled out a condom. I was grateful that I didn't have to ask him to use protection; he was smart enough to know it was the right thing to do. I closed my eyes, anticipating the way he'd feel as he slid inside of me. When he finally did, I gasped, unable to reign in the pleasure I felt.

It had been a long time, too long, since anyone had made me feel that good. Even before things had started to sour between me and Greg, he hadn't been able to do to me what Jeff was doing. With every thrust, he continued to caress me and kiss me, and he seemed to know the exact spots that gave me the most pleasure.

I climaxed a second time and then a third, before he did, his body trembling.

"So this is what it's like to sleep with a younger man," I teased as we lay in each other's arms after.

"What do you mean younger man?" Jeff sounded genuinely confused.

"Jesse never told you how old I am?" I asked, regretting that I'd brought it up. I knew Jeff was only twenty-four because Jesse mentioned it once, so somehow I'd assumed my age had also come up in a conversation between them.

"No. I figured you guys were around the same age since you both just finished college together."

He was in for a pretty big surprise. "I'm flattered you thought I was in my twenties, but you assumed wrong. I didn't start college right after high school. It took me a while to figure out what I wanted to do."

"So how old are you?" he said.

"Thirty-two," I replied, bracing myself for his reaction.

Jeff chuckled.

I nudged him playfully. "What's so funny?"

"When you referred to me as a younger man I was kind of hoping you'd tell me you were pushing forty. I've always wondered what it would be like to get a cougar into bed with me."

This time I elbowed him. "Not funny."

"Oh, come on. It was at least a little funny, wasn't it?"

"No," I said, refusing to admit that it was. I fell silent for a moment. "So you really thought I was younger?"

"If you're asking me if I think you look like you're thirty-two, then the answer is no. I really thought you were the same age as Jesse," he said. "But thirty-two or not, you're sexy as hell. I love everything about the way you look. Your face, your body, but especially your hair. I've always had a thing for wavy hair." He wound his finger around a lock.

"You've already gotten me into bed. There's no need for any more flattery."

"Now I'm the one who's offended. I don't offer compliments just to get women into bed."

"Then why do you offer them?" I asked.

"I like speaking my mind."

I sighed. Jeff was right. He didn't need to offer compliments to get a woman into bed. I'd known that from the moment we met a few months back at Jesse's graduation party. But we were both taken then. I was safe from his obvious talent at seduction then, not even registering his attraction to me. I reminded myself that that's all it was—an attraction. Merely physical, and I refused to let that thought bother me. I'd just had the best sex of my life. I resolved to be satisfied with that. I'd known what I was getting into when I agreed to come back to his place. And even though I wasn't really the one-night stand type, I had no regrets.

We talked for a little while longer, until I was too tired to keep my eyes open and drifted off to sleep in the crook of Jeff's arm.

Sometime later, I woke up. The clock said it was just after four in the morning. It occurred to me that if I got dressed and snuck out, there would be no morning-after awkwardness to deal with when the sun came up. I was fairly certain Jeff would appreciate the gesture, but I still nudged him, to make sure he was asleep before climbing out of bed. By leaving now, I'd avoid the whole, 'I'm not looking for a relationship' speech Jeff was bound to give me later, and save us both from the discomfort that came with that conversation.

I snuck out of his bedroom, picking up my underwear and dress from the floor. Once I finished dressing, I grabbed my purse from the coffee table and tiptoed out of his apartment.

Even at almost five o'clock in the morning it was easy enough to find a cab. By the time I reached home I was sleepy, but after leaving Bailey alone for so many hours he deserved a walk. After, I changed into pajamas and crawled into bed with Bailey curled up beside me like he'd done every night since Greg left. I closed my eyes, hoping for a few hours of sleep, but as I did, images of Jeff with his hands on me flooded my mind. I sighed. Did sex with him really have to be a one-time thing?

Eventually I managed to fall asleep, but not for long. I was awakened by my phone. The first time it rang, I ignored it. But right after the call went to voicemail it rang again. I reached for it, too groggy to check who was calling.

"Hello," I said, practically slurring my words.

"Where the hell are you?"

I sat up in bed, suddenly awake, startled both by the fact that Jeff was on the line and by the tone of his voice. I couldn't decide if he sounded worried or annoyed. "Jeff? How did you get my number?" I didn't remember giving it to him.

"I got it from Justin," he said.

"Wait. Aren't he and Jesse supposed to be on their honeymoon?"

"Never mind about that," Jeff said. "What time did you leave?"

"Um, around four."

"You didn't even leave a note," he said, his tone accusatory.

"I . . . I . . ." I had no idea what to say. "It was dark, and I don't know where you keep your paper and pens."

"You didn't have to leave like that," Jeff said, his tone softening. "I was hoping we could have breakfast together."

"I figured you probably had things to do in the morning. I didn't want to be in your way." I prayed I didn't sound as pathetic as I felt.

For a moment there was nothing but silence. Just as I was about to check if the call had dropped, Jeff spoke again. "Are you home?"

"Yeah."

"Well, at least I know you made it back safely. You didn't take the train, did you?"

"No, I caught a cab."

I didn't know the rules when it came to one-night stands, but I truly had expected that Jeff would appreciate not having to face me in the morning. Instead, he seemed bothered that I'd left. *Did that mean he cared?* I refused to let my mind go there. I wasn't going to be *that* girl. The one who slept with a guy and then couldn't stop thinking about him and wanting more than he could offer.

"Are you sure you're okay?" he said.

"Of course. Why wouldn't I be?" Did he expect that I'd be

full of regrets in the morning? I didn't want him thinking that way, so I added, "Thanks for last night."

"Glad to be of service," he said. His voice sounded strange, hollow.

I was tempted to ask if something was wrong, but instead I said good-bye and hung up, wondering how soon it would be before our paths crossed again.

Chapter 7
Confession Time

After getting off the phone with Jeff I tried falling back asleep, but it was no use. I kept replaying our conversation in my head. Eventually I decided that the only thing that would take my mind off of Jeff was getting out of bed and making myself busy. As I searched for something to wear, my engagement ring, which I'd taken off a few days ago and left on my dresser, caught my eye. I was supposed to be bringing it somewhere to see how much I could get for it. I dressed hurriedly and brought Bailey with me to the pawn shop that was a few blocks from my apartment.

I wound up getting a lot less money for that ring than I'd hoped to because the pawn shop broker said that even though the diamond was real, the quality was poor. Somehow that didn't really surprise me.

With the ring gone, my connection to Greg felt completely severed. We were really, truly, one hundred percent over. There was only one thing left to do. Break the news to my mom. I'd been dodging her calls for over a week and sooner or later she was bound to get suspicious, if she wasn't already. On my way back to my apartment I fished my phone out of my back pocket and dialed her number.

"So how was your friend's wedding? I take it that's the reason I haven't been able to get ahold of you," my mom asked. She knew I'd been Jesse's maid of honor.

"It was beautiful. Jesse looked amazing, and the botanical gardens in the fall are so gorgeous with all the leaves changing colors."

"That sounds wonderful. Perhaps you and Greg can have your wedding there. Although you probably don't want to have it at the same place as your friend."

"About that," I said, cutting my mom off. I took a deep breath and braced myself for her reaction to what I was about to say. "I don't know how to tell you this, but Greg and I are not getting married. We broke up."

"You what?" She sounded incredulous, which of course she would be since the last time we talked, Greg and I were still living together and engaged.

I explained about Greg moving out, but skipped over any mention of his new girlfriend, figuring my mom was probably shocked enough by my news as it was.

"I'm calling him right now and having a talk with him," she said in a huff. "He probably just got cold feet."

"Mom, no. Just leave it alone," I pleaded. This was why I'd put off telling her about the break-up for so long. I knew she'd get this way. "Greg and I are not getting back together."

"Oh, come on, Susan. You can't mean that. I know the two of you can sort things out. You've been together for too long to just give up now."

"I'm not the one who gave up. Greg did. And there's nothing to sort out. I'm sorry." I hated disappointing her; I still remembered how over the moon my mom had been when Greg and I got engaged.

"Have you even tried?"

I knew she meant well, which is why I did my best to explain that Greg and I had been sweeping our problems under the rug for so long that it had become too late to fix things, and calling him wouldn't make a difference. We'd both moved on.

Though it was on the tip of my tongue, I left out the part about the incredible sex I'd just had. I was dying to talk to someone about Jeff, but my mother was not the right person for that. I would have to wait until Jesse got back from her honeymoon. I shared a lot of things with my mom, but she was pretty old-fashioned, and would no doubt give me a lecture about jumping out of one's man's bed and into another's.

After I hung up, it felt like a load had been lifted off my shoulders. I was happy to have that over and done with, no matter how much I hated hearing the disappointment in my mother's voice. With my confession to Mom out of the way, I decided it was time to stop sitting around feeling sorry for myself and start moving on with my life. Which meant I needed to get serious about finding a real job.

I sat down in front of my computer and visited every career website I could think of. It wasn't until my eyes started to blur from too much screen time that I got up to take a break. But even then I didn't sit around idly. Instead I purged my apartment and cell phone of every photo of Greg. Then I rearranged my closet and dresser and got rid of the few things Greg had left behind. By the time I finished, I felt lighter, happier. Only one thing pressed on my mind. Jeff. I couldn't stop thinking about the way his lips felt on mine, about how gorgeously sculpted his body was and the way his hands felt caressing my skin. I wanted to pick up the phone and call him just to hear his voice, his jokes. No one made me laugh the way he did. But at the same time, I knew getting any closer to him would only lead to heartache.

~

A few days after Jesse got back from her honeymoon, we made plans to meet for coffee. She'd returned from the Caribbean gorgeously tanned and smiling. Seeing her like that made me happy. Just because things weren't going so hot for me these days didn't mean I couldn't be excited for my best friend.

"You look amazing," I said, after greeting her with a hug.

We ordered coffee and found two empty armchairs in the corner of the shop.

"I want to hear all about your honeymoon," I said, before bringing my steaming cup up to my lips.

Jesse described the resort she and Justin stayed at in the Bahamas. Somewhere in between her telling me about the clear blue ocean water and sipping cocktails on the beach as the sun went down, my mind drifted. I couldn't help it. I'd been dying to tell her about Jeff, so much so that it made it hard for me to focus on anything else.

"Earth to Susan," Jesse said, waving her hand back and forth in front of my face. I snapped out of my trance. "Is something wrong?" she asked.

"I slept with Jeff." As soon as the words came out I covered my mouth with my hand. I hadn't meant to blurt it out like that.

Jesse's eyes widened. She stared at me for a moment. "You slept with *who*?"

I bit my bottom lip and looked down, unable to meet her eyes. "You know, Jeff, your brother-in-law."

"When? Where? *Why?*" Jesse said, sounding far more in shock by my news than I'd expected her to. Although considering that she knew I wasn't really a one-night stand kind of girl I could see why.

"When was right after your wedding. Where was at his apartment. And as for why . . ." I wasn't exactly sure how to put the answer into words. "Besides the fact that he's gorgeous, I just felt like it. He's funny, and he makes me smile, and I didn't want to go back to an empty apartment."

Jesse's expression turned from shock to concern. "You do know he's not really a relationship type of guy. At least not anymore."

"I know, I know. You told me already," I said, setting my cup down on the little table between our chairs. "Sleeping with him was a one-time thing. I swear."

"So you haven't seen him again since?"

I shook my head and tried to hide my disappointment. I knew Jeff wasn't interested in getting to know me better, but I at least thought he'd try for another night together. The fact that he hadn't did nothing for my already-bruised ego.

"And you're okay with that?"

I shrugged. "Why wouldn't I be?"

Jesse eyed me suspiciously. She knew me better. But I was too embarrassed to admit the truth to myself, much less say the words out loud, that some small part of me had kind of hoped that Jeff would realize he was more interested in me than in being with a different woman every night.

Jesse shook her head. "Wow. I still can't believe it. My best friend and my brother-in-law." She smiled and leaned back in her chair. "Too bad you guys aren't dating for real."

"Why is it too bad?"

"Because if you guys got married, that would make us family. How awesome would that be?" Jesse asked, exuberantly. I loved how big her heart was.

"That's quite a leap," I said. "Besides, you heard Jeff at your wedding shower. He doesn't believe in spending the rest of his life with one person."

Jesse shook her head. "He wasn't always like that," she said. "I miss the old Jeff."

I was tempted to press her for more information, but I didn't. What was the point? Instead I changed the subject back to her honeymoon, listening attentively this time as she talked about walks on the beach and lazy afternoons lounging by the pool with Justin. Since I'd been following all of Jesse's posts on Facebook I already had a good mental image of everything she described.

When I arrived home later that afternoon I found my mom waiting for me in front of my building. Ever since I'd told her about my breakup with Greg, she'd been calling every day to tell me how worried she was about me being alone. I tried reminding her that before Greg had moved in I'd managed on my own without a problem. But I could tell she wasn't convinced. My mom liked to fret over me, probably because I was her only child.

If given the chance, I was sure she would've had more

children, but when I was still in kindergarten, my Dad died. He'd owned a convenience store and got shot and killed during an armed robbery. My mother never remarried. She was old-fashioned that way, believing there was only one man for her. Without any other children, or a husband, my mom doted on me, supplying me with so much love and attention that by the time I moved away from home I barely knew how to brew a pot of coffee on my own. But I'd learned. The one thing I had never mastered was cooking, which I was fairly certain was the reason for my mother's visit. She believed that a good meal could cure anything. With the way my mom cooked, I had no idea how she managed to maintain her perfect size-six figure. Luckily for us being petite just seemed to run in the family.

"You look like you've lost weight," she said, following me inside my apartment. "Have you been eating properly?"

"Yes, I've been eating, and no, I haven't lost any weight. It's probably just what I'm wearing."

"I worry about you all by yourself, dear. Why can't you call Greg and try to work things out?"

I knew that was coming, but found myself annoyed anyway. It wasn't like I'd chosen to end our relationship, and now she wanted me to grovel at his feet. That was not going to happen. "For the one hundredth time, Mom, there is nothing to work out. Greg and I are over."

"That's just your pride talking."

"No. It's not," I said, turning around to look at her squarely in the face. I didn't want to tarnish the image my mom had of Greg, but it seemed like there was only one way to finally get her to back off. "Greg has already moved on; he has a new girlfriend."

"How do you know that?"

She sounded as if she didn't believe me, so I told her about the woman who'd picked up Greg's phone the day after he moved out. My mother sat down, her shoulders slumped. I almost felt worse for her than I did for myself. She'd been hoping for a huge Italian wedding, a son-in-law, and grandchildren. None of which were going to happen. "Mom, I hate to break it to you, but not everyone is meant to get married and have kids."

That was the last thing she probably wanted to hear, but I figured it was high time she accepted that maybe her dreams of being a grandmother weren't going to materialize.

"I just want you to be happy," my mom said, reaching for my hands. "That's all."

"I am happy. I finally got my college degree, I've been substitute teaching and I still have my dog walking business," I said, trying to sound upbeat.

"I don't like the idea of you living here all alone. Why don't you move back home?"

"I'm not alone, Mom. I've got Bailey," I said. "Besides, the chances of me having any sort of love life as a thirty-something year old living with her mom are pretty slim."

She sighed, but didn't press the issue any further. Instead she got up from the couch, and asked me to join her in the kitchen. Just as I'd suspected—Mom had come to cheer me up with one of her amazing meals. I helped as she chopped and sautéed, taking in the amazing aroma of one of her home-cooked Italian dishes. This time it was chicken parmesan, one of my favorites. Something about the garlic and herbs my mom put in her tomato sauce combined with warm, melted cheese made everything better.

My mother stayed until she made sure I ate what she considered enough and washed all the dishes, despite my insistence that I was perfectly capable. I secretly loved that she still wanted to mother me even though I was an adult.

By the time my mom left we'd managed to make it through an entire meal and clean-up without another mention of Greg. As I gave my mom one final wave before closing the door behind her, I realized how grateful I was for that. It meant we were moving on and looking forward.

Chapter 8
Brunch

A few days later, I met Jesse and Justin at a trendy new restaurant that had just opened near Jesse's old neighborhood in Cobble Hill. After a short wait, the three of us were seated and handed menus. Seeing Justin sitting across the table made it impossible to not think about his brother. I found myself wondering how he was doing, and if he ever thought about me the way I thought of him.

I held off for as long as I could, but after the waiter took our orders, I couldn't help myself from casually asking, "So, how's Jeff doing?" I scolded myself for thinking about him, which I wasn't supposed to be doing, but apparently I wasn't very good at following my own advice.

"He's fine, I guess," Justin said. "I haven't really seen much of him since Jesse and I got back."

"I'm sure his legion of admirers keep him pretty busy." I felt like kicking myself for letting those words slip out. It was none of my business how he spent his time or who he spent it with.

"Yeah, well, it's about time he cut that Mr. Playboy shit out," Justin said, not mincing words. "Four months is long enough to get over an ex."

"Why did they break up anyway?" I asked, trying not to sound overly interested.

Justin and Jesse exchanged a wary glance. Of course they both knew why, but it seemed like they weren't sure whether or not to tell me.

"His ex cheated on him with one of his buddies," Justin finally said.

"You do know Jeff will kill you if he finds out you told anyone," Jesse said. She turned to look at me. "Outside of the two of us . . . well, now the three of us, nobody knows. He hasn't even told his parents what happened. He was pretty humiliated by the whole thing."

I shook my head. "I won't say a word." Justin's revelation shocked me. Why would anyone who was with a guy as incredible as Jeff cheat on him? "Do you know how he found out?"

"He came home early from work one day and found them together—*on his couch*!" Justin said.

"No way!" That explained why Jeff had such a poor opinion of relationships.

"Jeff was madly in love with Nina. He thought she was the one," Jesse added. "What she did broke him."

Justin nudged Jesse with his elbow. Following his line of vision she looked up toward the restaurant's entrance. I turned to see what had captured their attention. It was Jeff. He was headed over to our table.

"You didn't tell me he'd be here," I whispered to Jesse.

"That's because I didn't know," she replied.

"Did I not tell you I invited Jeff?" Justin asked.

My face heated as Jeff made his way over to us. I hadn't

expected to see him and I found myself totally unprepared for the rush I felt inside. My tongue, for some strange reason, stopped functioning. I knew I was supposed to say something, but I couldn't come up with a thing.

Finally Jeff broke the awkward silence. "It's nice to see you, Sue. You look good."

I looked good? What did he mean by that? I ran a hand through my unruly hair and managed a weak smile. "Thanks. You do, too," I said, knowing I sounded stupid. Jeff wore jeans and a polo shirt in blue that brought out the color of his eyes. He looked model handsome. It just wasn't fair that he was so damn gorgeous.

The fluttery feeling in my chest made it hard to do anything more than pick at the breakfast I'd ordered. While Jeff chatted with his brother and Jesse, I sat there mostly silent, trying to come up with something witty to say, but never finding the right words.

After a while, Jeff turned to me, "You're awfully quiet today."

"I…I didn't know you were going to be here," I said, realizing I sounded like a tongue-tied teenager trying to talk to her crush.

"Justin forgot to mention you were coming," Jesse said. I kind of figured that. If she'd known Jeff was going to be here, she would've told me.

Jeff frowned. "Is it a problem that I'm here?"

"No." I shook my head. "Of course not. It's just a surprise, that's all."

Jeff stabbed a piece of pancake with his fork. "Funny thing is, I actually didn't know you were going to be here either."

"Didn't I tell you?" Justin said. I got the feeling he'd set this whole thing up. I was going to have to get Jesse to tell her husband to stop trying to be a matchmaker.

"Well, your brother is married to my best friend," I said, "so I guess I'm bound to run into you every now and then."

"I like the idea of running into you, so I'm fine with it," Jeff said with a wink. Was he back to flirting or did he actually mean what he'd just said?

"So what have you been up to since the wedding?" I asked, hoping that somewhere in his answer I could glean why he hadn't called or even bothered with a text since the last time we talked. Of course I hadn't called or texted either, but I was sure my reasons weren't the same as his.

"Nothing much," he replied casually. "Work mostly."

My mind went blank again. Once more I tried to think of something to say, thankfully Jesse saved me from having to come up with the right words by asking Jeff how his last business trip had gone.

When the four of us were done eating, I breathed a silent sigh of relief. All I had to do was get through paying the check. Then I planned on making an excuse about needing to get back home right away to walk Bailey. Just being around Jeff was playing with my mind. He was just as gorgeous, funny, polite, and totally out of my reach as ever and I was desperately attracted to him, which would've been fine if the attraction was only physical, but it was definitely more than that. At least for me.

When the waiter finally came over to our table to hand each of us our checks, Jeff intercepted mine.

"I got this," he said.

My cheeks heated, again. "You don't have to do that."

"I know I don't have to, but I want to."

I could feel Jesse and Justin's eyes on us and decided to let it go. After the credit card receipts were all signed, the four of us walked outside together.

"I've got a ton of stuff to do today, so I should really get going," I announced, ready to make my escape.

"Let me walk you to the train station," Jeff said as Jesse gave me a quick goodbye hug.

"It's only a block away," I told him, "I'm sure I can manage."

I spotted Justin tugging on his wife's hand out of the corner of my eye and got the sneaking suspicion that he wanted to leave me and Jeff to talk privately. "We'll see you two later," Jesse said, lacing her fingers through her husband's. "Justin and I are going to take a cab back into the city."

Justin's lips curled into a smile that pretty much confirmed my hunch that he had planned this brunch as some sort of double date. Why would he do that when he knew what a player his brother was?

After Jesse and Justin walked away, Jeff turned to me. "You and I should talk."

"About what?" I asked, trying to sound aloof, which wasn't easy with the way he was making my heart flutter.

"I don't know." Jeff ran a hand through his hair. "Maybe about how awkward things are between us now. I didn't want it to be like this."

"The thing is, I'm not really a one-night-stand type of girl, so I don't know the rules about how to act after," I said as we walked slowly down the street toward the nearest train station.

"Maybe it was a bad idea. I mean, you're not just some girl.

You're my sister-in-law's best friend, and I don't want you thinking I'm some pervy guy who has a new girl in his apartment every night. It's not like that."

"You did say more than once that you don't believe in long-term relationships."

"I don't. But that doesn't mean I'm sleeping with every girl in the five boroughs."

"Yeah well, Staten Island is kind of a commute, so I understand."

Jeff smiled. "See, that's what I mean. You're one of the only people I know who has a weird sense of humor like I do."

I smiled back. "What are you trying to say?"

"That I want to still at least be friends. Just because we slept together doesn't mean we can't be, does it?"

"Why would you think that I don't want to be your friend?" Had I accidentally said something to make him believe that wasn't what I wanted? Although, the more I thought about it, I wondered if a friendship with Jeff was possible. Especially if I couldn't figure out a way to stop the feelings I'd begun to have.

"You snuck out of my apartment without a word. And it's been two weeks since then, and you haven't called."

I frowned. Had he really expected me to call? "You haven't either."

"Yes, I did. I called you the morning after," he said. "So that means it was your turn."

I couldn't help my nervous laughter. "Do you realize how silly the two of us sound?"

He smiled. "Are you calling me silly?"

"Maybe a little."

Jeff reached for my hand. "Instead of going home, maybe we can take a walk over to the park and just hang out for a bit."

"Normally I'd say yes, but I've got like five dogs that need to be walked, and if I don't get to them soon I'm going to have a mess on my hands."

Jeff furrowed his brows. "You have five dogs?"

"They're not mine," I explained. "At least most of them aren't. I have one dog, the rest I walk for other people."

"So you're a teacher and a professional dog walker. Nice."

"It's fun." I shrugged. "I've always been an animal lover."

"I could walk them with you. I really like dogs, too. Always wanted one as a kid, but, you know my mom. There was no way she was going to let anything that shed inside our home."

I laughed. "Then your mother would die if she saw my apartment."

"Good thing she's not invited." Jeff flashed me another one of his irresistible smiles.

"All right," I said, chewing on my bottom lip to keep myself from returning his smile, knowing I'd probably look goofy, instead of sexy like he did. I did not want him to know the effect he had on me. I was starting to realize, with dismay, that my inability to resist Jeff's charms was probably going to be my downfall. "You can come."

Chapter 9
Friends With Benefits

"You live above a bar?" Jeff asked as I stopped in front of my building to fish my keys out of my bag.

After unlocking the door I pushed it open. "You say it like there's something wrong with that."

"It doesn't get noisy in your apartment?"

"I'm on the top floor, so not really," I said, leading the way.

He followed me up the two flights of stairs to my apartment. Bailey greeted me first, then Jeff, excitedly jumping up and wagging his tail. "Down," I instructed. I'd never trained Bailey out of his exuberant greetings because I liked them, even though I knew not everybody else necessarily did. "Sit." Bailey did as commanded, and I quickly rewarded him by giving him a treat.

Jeff crouched down in front of Bailey and started stroking the top of his head and scratching under his chin. Bailey loved the attention. He lay down and then flipped over on his back for a belly rub, something he only did with people he liked.

I chuckled. "You're so silly, Bailey." I reached for his collar and leash, which hung from a hook behind the door, and clasped it around his neck. As much as Bailey loved tummy rubs, he loved going outside more, so he got up and followed as I led him down the stairs.

"Do you mind if I walk him?" Jeff asked, reaching for the leash as we headed down the block.

"You sure?"

"I told you, I love dogs."

I smiled. So Jeff really was a dog lover. As if I needed another reason to like him more than I already did.

I handed him Bailey's leash, and the two of them trailed behind me, stopping every few minutes for Bailey to sniff or get his head scratched by a passerby. He was a beautiful dog, with thick golden fur, so people often asked if they could pet him and Bailey absolutely adored the attention.

After I reached my first client's apartment, I unlocked the door to his house, got his dog, a Dalmatian named Roxy, on a leash, and locked the door behind me.

"People give you the keys to their house?" Jeff asked as if it was the strangest thing in the world.

"It's no different than giving them to a housekeeper." I was fairly certain Jeff's parents did not clean their own home. "Besides, I've known my clients for a long time. Before I went to college I worked at an animal hospital a few blocks away as a vet tech. That's how I got to know all these dog owners."

"So do you do this every day?"

"Just on weekends. It was too hard to do it every day when I was taking classes, and now I substitute teach sometimes during the week, which makes my schedule unpredictable," I explained. "But even though I only dog walk on weekends, finding clients has never been a problem. People like to get out of town, or they have jobs that make them work Saturdays and Sundays."

"How very business-minded of you," Jeff said. "Although what I don't get is why someone would get a dog in the first place if they don't have enough time to walk it. Seems kind of sad."

"Not at all. Just because someone is super busy with work doesn't mean they don't want the kind of companionship that you get from having a pet," I said. "A lot of my clients work crazy hours. They're doctors or firefighters, and they want someone waiting for them when they get home after a long day."

"Hmm. When you put it like that, maybe I should think about getting one." He leaned down to give Bailey another scratch under his chin.

Three houses later I had all four dogs that needed walking, plus Bailey. We headed to Shore Road Park for some off-the-leash playtime. With Jeff helping, the dogs got plenty of exercise. He seemed like he was actually having fun, which I couldn't help but adore. Greg thought of anything dog-related as a chore, but to me, passing the day outside, watching the dogs play, relaxed me. In another month it would be super cold; I wanted to be outside as much as possible until then.

I kept glancing at Jeff out of the corner of my eye as he tossed balls for the dogs to chase after, trying to piece together everything I'd learned about him since we'd first met. By the time we headed back home I was no closer to figuring him out. What I did know was that no matter how badly I wanted him to be someone other than the player he professed himself to be, hanging onto the hope that I could change him was foolish. He'd make a great friend, and an amazing lover, but as a boyfriend he'd leave my heart in shreds.

I sighed and walked over to Jeff, reaching for his hand. He turned to look at me. "We should get going," I said.

After walking the dogs back to their owners' homes, Jeff and I headed back to my apartment.

"Do you want to get a drink first?" Jeff asked.

I hesitated. I knew all the bartenders who worked there—so did Greg—and I was certain that whoever was on today would wonder why I was having a drink with someone other than the man they still believed was my fiancé. I hadn't been to the bar since Greg moved out because I wasn't up for the inevitable round of 'how's Greg' questions that always accompanied a trip there. But sooner or later I was going to have to deal with it, so why not today? And at least with Jeff beside me, no one would ask overly prying questions.

"Okay. Let me just drop Bailey off first."

After bringing my dog back upstairs, Jeff and I took seats at the bar. The bartender, a friend of mine named Donna, walked over. "Hey Susan," she said, reaching across the bar to give me a hug and a kiss on my cheek. "Long time, no see. Where have you been?"

"It's a long story," I said, hoping she'd figure out that now was not the time for me to tell it. Donna and I had been friends since I'd moved into the neighborhood, and although I wasn't as close to her as I was to Jesse, she did help me out whenever I spent the night at my mom's by making sure Bailey got walked and fed.

"You're okay, though, right?"

I nodded. "Yeah, I'm fine. Just been busy," I said. "What about you?"

"Same here." She glanced at Jeff. "Do you two want menus or are you guys just grabbing a drink?"

"Just drinks," I said, figuring that like me, Jeff was still full from brunch.

"So who's your friend?" Donna asked, studying him.

"Sorry," I said, realizing I'd forgotten to make introductions. "Donna, this is Jeff."

She smiled at him as they shook hands. "So what are you having?"

"Hmmm. Maybe you should order first," Jeff said to me. "I'm not really sure what I'm in the mood for."

"I already know what Susan's getting," Donna said.

"I pretty much always order the same thing," I explained.

"Well then, I'll just take whatever Susan's having."

"Okay. Two Guinnesses then. Be right back with those."

While Jeff and I drank our beers, a few more people from the neighborhood walked over to say hello and, like Donna, ask me where I'd been. They all eyed Jeff suspiciously, probably wondering what I was doing with him when I was supposed to be engaged to Greg. It made having a full conversation with him practically impossible.

"You're like a local celebrity," Jeff teased.

"When you live in the same neighborhood for a few years, you get to know people."

"I don't think that's it," Jeff said. "You're just one of those people who are impossible not to like."

"I don't know about that," I replied, trying to hide my smile. Being complimented was usually a good thing, but with Jeff I wasn't sure how much of what he said was real and how much was part of his playboy routine.

After finishing our beers, Jeff paid our tab and left a generous tip for Donna.

"Do you want me to walk you to the train station or do you remember how to get there on your own?" I asked as we headed outside.

"Can I say bye to Bailey first?" The pleading look on his face made it impossible to say no despite the voice in my head screaming at me that inviting him upstairs was asking for trouble.

"He'd be pretty devastated if you didn't," I replied sarcastically, hiding my nervousness with humor.

"We wouldn't want that." I caught a grin on Jeff's face before turning around to head up the stairs. We found Bailey lying on the couch, probably tuckered out from his time at the dog park earlier. Jeff sat beside him, scratching his belly and petting the top of his head until the sound of me emptying a cup of kibble into his dog bowl sent him flying off the couch.

"Come sit," Jeff said, looking over his shoulder at me.

"I thought all you wanted to do was say bye to my dog. I'm beginning to think you've got ulterior motives for inviting yourself over."

"I would never," he protested.

"You can stay," I said, as I sat beside him, burying my sweaty palms under my thighs, "as long as you don't put sports on. The minute I see ESPN on my TV, you're outta here."

Jeff chuckled. "Then it's a good thing I'm not into sports."

"Really?" How was this guy even possible? "Then how did you get those washboard abs of yours?"

He smiled and cocked his head to the side. "You like my abs?"

"Not fair, answering a question with a question," I said,

wishing I had some sort of magic that could take back words that were already said.

"Okay, you got me. I don't like watching sports on TV. It's boring. I don't get why so many guys are into it. But I do like working out, and I'm part of a soccer league."

Holy moly, I literally had the most perfect guy on the planet in my apartment, sitting next to me on my couch. He loved dogs, was great in bed, gorgeous, had a good job, loved playing sports but hated watching them. There was only one problem, and unfortunately, it was a pretty big one. Jeff wasn't relationship material. Life could be really unfair sometimes.

"It's your turn now," he said.

I frowned. "My turn for what?"

"To answer my question."

"You mean the one about me liking your abs?"

"That's the one."

I shrugged, "Yeah, they're okay."

"Just okay?" Jeff lifted his shirt halfway up and stared down at his perfect six-pack. "I guess I'm going to need to do more crunches."

I turned away so that I wasn't gawking at Jeff's amazing physique, grabbed the remote, switched the TV on, and started flipping through channels. When I got to the Food Network, Jeff grabbed the remote from my hands.

"I love this show," he said.

"*Diners, Drive-Ins and Dives*? Are you kidding me?"

"You've never watched it?"

"Not for more than five minutes. I've never really been into watching other people eat."

"Just look at that guy's face," Jeff said, pointing to the TV just as the host shoved a giant sandwich dripping with grease into his mouth. "Now that is a man who truly loves his job."

The more I watched, the more I had to admit that there was something infectious about the joy Guy Fieri got from the food he was eating. By the time the show was over I was half-tempted to book a ticket to Atlanta and try out the restaurant he'd been raving about.

"I can't believe you have me watching the Food Network when I'm supposed to be sending out resumes," I said after watching the second back-to-back episode of the show.

Jeff clicked the TV off and turned toward me. "How about we make a trade?"

I furrowed my brows. "What kind of trade?"

He reached for my hands, sending my heart on a wild rollercoaster ride through my chest. "I'll help you with your job hunt, if you let me kiss you again."

My insides twisted into knots. "Um, what happened to us just being friends?"

"We can still be friends." His lips curled into that irresistible smile of his. "Friends with benefits."

Before I had a chance to protest, to tell him I didn't think I was capable of a relationship like that, he moved in closer, pulled me to him and pressed his lips on mine. All logical thought, all reason, melted into a giant, shapeless puddle. I wasn't supposed to kiss him back, but I did anyway. I wasn't supposed to let him undress me, but I couldn't help myself. When it came to Jeff, I was over the moon and there was no turning back.

Chapter 10
A Sleepover

Sex with Jeff the first time had been incredible, but the second time—and then the third—was even more amazing.

In the morning I woke up groggy, thanks to Jeff waking up in the middle of the night with a rock-hard erection. He wasn't one for quickies. The man liked to take his time, making sure I got the same amount of pleasure from him that he got from me. It made for one unforgettable night, but also one tired, and sore, woman the next morning.

I felt him stir beside me and checked to see if he'd opened his eyes yet.

"Good morning, beautiful," he said, turning on his side and planting a kiss on my shoulder.

I slid my arms around him and then glanced at the bedside clock. It was still morning, but barely. "You, mister, were supposed to help me find a job, not keep me in bed until almost noon," I teased.

"Is it that late already?" Jeff said. "No wonder I'm so hungry. Or . . ." He kissed my forehead. "It could be you that's got my stomach rumbling."

"Me?"

"I did burn quite a few calories through the night," Jeff teased.

I smiled. "Someone's got to help you stay in shape."

"I'm up for round three if you are." Jeff's eyes sparkled as he smiled back.

"Hmm. I don't know. Bailey might just change his mind about you if you keep me in bed all day."

"Okay, okay. How about this? We go take Bailey for his walk, then you let me take you to breakfast and after I'll show you what a master job hunter I can be."

"Another trade? How many of those am I going to have to make before I can actually get some work done?"

"Tell you what. I'll let you pick the restaurant."

I shook my head, realizing that there weren't many things I could say no to when it came to Jeff Lambert. He had me totally under his spell. "Fine, it's a deal," I said, ecstatic to have more time with him despite my silly attempt at playing hard to get. Not that it mattered, I was fairly certain Jeff could see through my jokes since we seemed to have a similar sense of humor. I threw back the covers, got out of bed and headed for the bathroom. I was starving, but before we went anywhere I needed a hot shower.

I got the water to the right temperature and stepped into the tub, looking up at the shower head so I could feel the water rain down on my face. Just as I reached for the soap I felt Jeff behind me. His arms circled my waist and his erection dug into my back. I turned around to face him and wrapped my arms around his back. As he pulled me closer, the feel of his skin on mine sent my heart into overdrive again.

"I thought you were hungry," I said.

"I decided I was hungrier for you than for breakfast." He kissed me hard and deep and then his lips traveled down to my neck.

"Mmmm." The feel of him drove me wild. Suddenly I didn't care about breakfast anymore, either. His hands cupped my breasts and then his tongue teased my nipples. I moaned wildly, loving every caress, every kiss.

Jeff took the soap in his hands and lathered every inch of me, lingering over my breasts and between my legs. When he was done he took the shampoo, then the conditioner and rubbed it into my hair, slowly massaging my scalp and neck.

After rinsing my hair, I returned the favor. Jeff gasped as I took his erection in my hands. He leaned forward, turning the water off before lifting me into his arms and carrying me back to bed. I moaned as he eased inside me, arching my back to get as close to him as I could.

When we finally made it out of my apartment, it was way past breakfast time. Not that either of us really minded. We brought Bailey on a walk before grabbing lunch. True to his word, after we returned to my apartment, Jeff sat down in front of the tiny desk that was wedged into the corner of my living room and opened up my laptop. He combed through website after website for teaching jobs that I could apply for.

"I wish tomorrow was Sunday again," Jeff said after we finished searching every possible job opportunity we could think of.

It was starting to get dark outside and it suddenly dawned on me that that meant I'd just spent over twenty-four hours with

Jeff. I would have loved another night with him, too, but that wasn't going to be possible. "I actually have a sub job tomorrow, which means I need to get some sleep tonight."

He pulled me onto his lap. "I'll be out of town for work next weekend, so I won't be able to see you until I get back."

"Really? Where are you headed?"

"Chicago." He kissed me, and as he did, his hand traveled up the back of my shirt. "I wish I didn't have to go. I'd much rather spend another weekend with you."

"Hmmm. Two weekends in a row with the same girl? If you're not more careful, you're going to put your player status in serious jeopardy."

Jeff withdrew his hand from under my shirt rather abruptly and scooted me off his lap. "Well, then, I guess it's a good thing I'll be out of town," he said. I couldn't tell if he was joking or not. Maybe because my heart had just dropped. I'd wanted a different response, and silently scolded myself for getting my hopes up. He stood and crossed the room, collecting his keys and cell phone from the side table in the living room.

"Will you be too busy for a phone call from me?" I asked, hating myself for sounding so desperate. I'd been having so much fun that I'd almost forgot about our whole friends with benefits arrangement.

Jeff turned to look at me. "You were planning on calling me?" he asked, seeming surprised by my question.

I nodded. "Why wouldn't I? We're friends, right?"

"That would be nice," he said. "I'd really like it if you did."

I walked over to him and planted a kiss on his cheek. He stared at me, and for a moment it looked like he wanted to say something. Instead, he turned to leave. As soon as he closed the door behind him I ran into my bedroom and looked out the window, waiting until he emerged from my building. After he did I stayed glued to my window, watching him as he walked down the street toward the train station, hating that I wasn't sure when I'd see him again.

Chapter 11
Making a Fool Out of Myself

I held out until Wednesday before calling Jeff, hoping that he'd call first, but he never did. When he didn't answer, my heart sank. The next day when he called back and I saw his name displayed on the screen of my phone I couldn't help the way my heart fluttered—even with my mom sitting across the kitchen table from me. As I pressed the phone to my ear, I got up to pour myself another cup of coffee

"I'm getting back earlier than I thought I would," he said. "My flight's tomorrow. I'd really like to see you."

"Sure." I looked over my shoulder, worried my mother was eavesdropping. "Sounds good."

"Great. I'll call you when I get back then."

"I take it that wasn't Greg you were talking to," my mom said after I hung up.

I frowned. "How many times have I told you that the two of us are over?"

"It's not unheard of to remain friends. You were together for a long time."

"Right, like I'd be friends with someone who cheated on me,

broke up with me through a note, and left without bothering to pay his share of the rent. Whatever bridge the two of us might have had, Greg burned it to the ground."

She shook her head. "I'm so disappointed in him." Even though I'd moved on, my mother still seemed upset by my break-up. She'd come by with a box of cannoli to cheer me up. I didn't need it, but I got the feeling she did, and I wasn't about to turn down Italian pastries or an excuse to brew another pot of coffee.

"Yeah, well that makes the two of us," I muttered.

"So there are no other fellows on the dating horizon for you?"

My mother sounded so optimistic, like she was sure I had a dozen suitors lined up to take Greg's place. For a moment I was tempted to tell her about Jeff, but she wouldn't be interested in hearing about a man I had no future with. I could already hear her lecturing me about wasting my time instead of searching for a husband and someone who'd make a good father. So instead of mentioning him, I just said, "Nope."

"I've heard that quite a few people have had success with dating websites like *Match.com*. Have you thought about trying something like that?"

For a second I thought she was joking, but the expression on my mom's face was serious. "No, Mom. Right now the only thing I'm using the internet for is to find a job."

"Perhaps you should think about broadening your horizons."

"I can't believe you, of all people, are encouraging me to date practical strangers."

It was so unlike my mother, who wouldn't even let me take the subway on my own until I was halfway through high school.

"What would you say if I told you that I've been dating

someone for the past few months," she said, "someone I met online?"

My eyes widened. "I'd say who snatched my mom and replaced her with an exact lookalike?"

She smiled. "Perhaps you're being a tad overdramatic."

"You're serious?"

"It was time, Susan. After your father died, I truly believed I'd never give my heart to anyone else, but I got tired of being alone."

Still stunned, it took me a moment to collect my thoughts. "So what's this guy's name?" I finally asked.

"His name is Frank," she said. "And I was hoping to introduce you to him at Thanksgiving dinner in a few weeks."

I had so not been expecting that. Not only was my mom involved with a guy she met on a dating website, but apparently things were serious between the two of them. For years I'd been encouraging my mom to start dating again, I just never thought she'd actually do it.

~

The next day Jeff texted me from the airport in Chicago to tell me he was about to board his flight back to New York. After his plane landed, he called. "Are you home?" he asked.

"I am. Why?"

"Because I just sent a cab to your place. I want you to come over."

"How presumptuous of you," I said, falling back on humor like I often did when I talked to him, partly because that's what I did when I was nervous, and partly because Jeff seemed to enjoy the way we joked with each other. "What if I already had plans?"

"Do you?"

I paused before answering, "No. Unless watching TV with Bailey counts."

"Then spend the night," he said "I've missed you."

I felt torn. A part of me couldn't wait to see Jeff again, but another part of me wanted to come clean and admit that our friends with benefits arrangement wasn't really what I wanted. How had I let things get so confused? Our one-night stand was supposed to be just that, a one-time thing. And then he'd asked to be friends. I should have told him then that I didn't think it was a good idea, but then I would have had to explain why.

"All right," I said. "Will I have enough time to pack a change of clothes?"

"The cabbie will wait. The most important thing is that he brings you to me."

Jeff could say the sweetest things sometimes, but I reminded myself they were just words. Reading more into them was foolish.

It took me a few minutes to gather the things I needed. I ran downstairs just as the cab pulled up to the curb. When I arrived at Jeff's building, I took the elevator up to his floor. My heart flip-flopped as I lifted my hand to knock on his door. As soon as he opened it, he pulled me inside and into his arms. He pressed his lips on mine. As his kisses became more urgent, I pulled away. It wasn't that I didn't want him, but something about coming all the way to his place just to jump straight into bed with him didn't feel right, and by the way his hands caressed me, it seemed like that's where things were headed.

"What's wrong?" he asked.

"Nothing," I said, feeling flustered as I backed away from him. "It's just that, well, maybe we could talk for a bit first."

"Sorry," Jeff said. "I just missed you, that's all."

"Me, or the benefits I come with?" As soon as those words came out I wished I could take them back.

"I thought you liked those benefits as much as I did." He inched closer, snaking his arms around my waist and planting soft kisses on my neck.

"I do," I said, afraid to confess that I wanted more, nervous that if I did, I'd scare him off. "But how about we get some dinner first? You can tell me all about your trip."

"Dinner?" he said. "Of course. It's almost six. You must be hungry. I don't know why I didn't think of that."

"Apparently, you had your mind on other things," I said biting my lower lip as I glanced down at the bulge in his pants.

Jeff flashed me that wicked grin of his. "I still do, but that can wait until after we eat." He grabbed his jacket and keys and the two of us headed outside. We stopped for dinner at a Thai restaurant a few blocks away.

"Tell me what you're thinking about," Jeff said after we'd given the waitress our orders. He must've noticed how quiet I'd been since we had left his apartment.

"I've been kind of wondering something, but I'm not sure if it's safe to ask you about it."

"Well, now you're going to have to, because you've got me curious."

I'd been nervously wiping beads of condensation off my water glass, but stopped to look up and meet his eyes. "When we first met, you had a girlfriend. What happened to her?" I asked, careful not to reveal anything Justin or Jesse had told me.

"What happened is we broke up," Jeff said, with an unmistakable trace of bitterness in his voice.

"Yeah, but why?" I pressed.

He took a sip of water before replying. "Because humans are meant to be polyamorous; they're not meant to be with one person for the rest of their life. It's not natural."

My heart sank. I wasn't sure which was worse, his words, or that he'd said them in such a detached, almost robotic way. Like a fool I'd hoped that I could get him to change his mind about relationships and that he found me special. Apparently, I was dead wrong. "Is that really how you feel?" I managed to choke out after he was done with his anthropology lesson.

He shook his head. "I don't know what I feel anymore. All I know is that's what my ex told me after I caught her fucking my friend, Jake, on our couch. Nina's one of the smartest girls I've ever known, so I figure she must know what she's talking about."

"So wait, let me get this straight. Your ex cheats on you, tells you humans weren't meant to be monogamous, and then you decide she's right and start screwing half of Manhattan?"

Jeff laughed, probably thinking I was making a joke even though I was being dead serious. "Nowhere near half," he said. "I mean, I'm not going to lie; I've hooked up with some girls after Nina and I broke-up, but it was mostly because getting drunk and taking some random girl home helped me forget what an idiot I was for believing in all that true love crap."

The more he talked, the worse I felt. "So that's what this is all about," I said, pointing back and forth between the two of us.

"I'm meant to help your forget about your ex."

"No." Jeff reached for my hand, flashing me that flirtatious smile of his at the same time. Apparently he didn't get that I was upset. "I'm meant to help you forget about yours."

What?! He took me to bed out of pity? I would have snatched my hand back, but right at that moment the waitress came with our dinners. Jeff started to eat. I just sat there, not knowing what to think, or say, or do. The only thing I did know was that my appetite had vanished.

"What's wrong?" Jeff asked, looking up at me. "How come you're not eating?"

"I'm not hungry anymore." I took the napkin off my lap, laid it on the table, and managed to swallow the lump in my throat. "And I'm not feeling very well right now." I got up.

Jeff grabbed my hand. "Where are you going?"

I pulled it away from him and stormed out of the restaurant, biting the inside of my cheek to keep from crying. He followed and I sped up until I was practically running down the street. When he called my name I pretended not to hear him and kept going. Tears started to roll down my cheeks and they didn't stop during the entire train ride back to Bay Ridge.

By the time I made it back home I was too tired to do anything other than get under my covers and go to sleep with Bailey pressed up against me.

Chapter 12
Jesse Gets a Job

I spent the next day in a daze, walking the dogs, making a sandwich I had no appetite to eat, and ignoring Jeff's calls. Then, to avoid more mental and emotional torture than I could stand, I got back into bed.

On Monday I had a job interview that didn't go well. I could tell from the start that they wanted someone with more experience than I had. I returned home, defeated and depressed at the realization that it wasn't just my personal life that sucked, but my professional one too.

A few hours later I got a call from Jesse. Anticipating how much better I'd feel after venting to her, I picked up the phone.

"You will never guess what happened," Jesse practically squealed right after I said hello.

"You're right, I won't," I said, curious what had her so excited.

"I got a job!"

Her news caught me by surprise, and came at the exact worst time. I reminded myself that Jesse had no idea about the disappointing interview I'd had earlier. "You got a job?" I managed to choke out. Suddenly I felt nauseous. "Where?"

"At a middle school near the Village," she said, brimming with excitement. "It's like my dream job. It doesn't start until after winter break is over, but still. A teaching job smack dab in the middle of the school year. Do you know how hard that is to get? I still can't believe it."

Of course I knew how hard a mid-year teaching job was to find, because I'd been desperately searching for one myself. Still, I wasn't about to let my failure keep me from being happy for my friend. "That's great, Jesse. Congratulations. I'm so happy for you," I said, and I truly was, but I heard my voice crack as the words came out. For some completely insane reason I felt like I was on the verge of tears. I choked down the lump in my throat and continued. "Is Justin taking you out to celebrate?"

"You sound strange, Susan. Is everything okay?"

"Yeah, fine. I think I might be coming down with a stomach bug, though." The words were barely out of my mouth when I felt a sudden urge to throw up. "I gotta go."

I dropped the phone before running into the bathroom, ready to empty the contents of my stomach into the toilet. Despite the fact that I felt like puking, nothing actually came up. I slumped down onto the floor and sat there hugging my bent knees with my back pressed against the wall. The last thing I needed on top of everything else was to be sick.

I took a few deep breaths and eventually managed to get up and drag myself over to the couch. My phone rang again, but I felt too sick to my stomach to talk so I ignored it. It dinged a minute later to tell me I had a text. It was from Jesse.

I'm coming over.

In the mood I was in, I knew I wouldn't be good company,

so I called her back to tell her I was fine, but probably contagious. When she didn't pick up I left her a text but she rang my doorbell a half hour later anyway. Damn subway reception. I buzzed her in and unlocked my door so she could let herself in.

"So do you really just have a stomach bug or is something else going on?"

I looked over my shoulder while Jesse took off her jacket and hung it on a hook near the entrance. "Something else like what?"

"I don't know, that's why I'm asking," she said, taking a seat beside me.

I shook my head. "This just hasn't been my day, that's all."

"Is it Greg? Have you heard from him again?"

"Oh, God no."

"Then what is it?"

My shoulders slumped and I bowed my head, resting my chin in the palm of my hand. "I don't want to talk about my problems. At least not right now," I said. "I'd rather toast to your new job."

Jesse put her hand on my shoulder. I lifted my head to look at her. "No toasting until you tell me what's going on."

"It's like I said. My stomach doesn't feel good." Despite the skeptical look on Jesse's face, I wasn't lying to her. It still hadn't settled.

"I know you, Susan. There's something you're not telling me."

"It's just been a shitty few weeks," I said, shaking my head. "My love life is crappy, and I can't find a job. I'll probably spend the rest of my life walking other people's dogs and living alone above some stupid bar."

"First of all, you will find a job," Jesse said. "And second of all, you and Greg just broke up. You need to give yourself some time to get over him first."

"I'm over Greg. *He's* not the problem."

Jesse frowned. "Then who is?"

I pulled at a loose thread on one of the couch cushions. I didn't want to tell her about Jeff. She'd warned me that he wouldn't be interested in anything serious and I'd been an idiot to hope that I could change his mind. But I needed to talk to someone about him, even if that someone was his sister-in-law. "Jeff," I confessed. "Jeff is the problem."

"It's funny you mention him," she said. "Justin was just telling me the other day that he thinks Jeff really likes you."

"Well, he's wrong. The only thing he likes is having sex with me."

Jesse's eyes widened. "Are you saying you guys had sex again? I thought you said sleeping with him was a one-time thing."

"It was supposed to be. But somehow he invited himself over and one thing led to another."

Jesse stared at me like she was trying to process the information I'd just given her. "You've got feelings for him." When I didn't deny it, she added, "I knew it."

I wasn't surprised that she'd figured it out. I'd always been sort of an open-book person. "I know what you're going to say. You tried to warn me about him and I didn't listen."

"He used to be different," she said. "I think all he needs is to find the right person."

"That's not going to happen. When Jeff's ex cheated she somehow managed to convince him that what she did was normal, that people aren't really meant to be in monogamous relationships. That's why he's been with so many women since they broke up," I explained. "But do you want to know what's really crazy? Jeff thinks I'm like him. He thinks that I slept with him to get over Greg, just like he went around sleeping with a bunch of girls to get over his ex."

"How do you know that?"

I told Jesse about my dinner date with Jeff, and the conversation we'd had.

"I get why you were upset, but I can't believe you just ran off without telling him why."

When she phrased it like that I had to admit my reaction that night had been a bit extreme. "It sounds crazy, I know. I have no idea what came over me."

"When you really like someone, they have a way of making you act kind of crazy," she said. I had to smile at that. She was exactly right. I'd seen her act plenty crazy when she and Justin first got together. Apparently, now it was my turn. "Jeff doesn't really talk to me about his personal life, but I do know that you're different than the other girls he's been sleeping with since he and Nina broke up. Most of them were practically strangers to him, one-night stands, women he never planned on seeing or talking to again. You're my best friend. He wouldn't treat you that way. He knows I'd kill him."

I shook my head. "That's what I tried telling myself at first, but after what he said the other night I don't think so."

"I really think you should call him and tell him how you're feeling." I gave her an incredulous look. "Hear me out," she said. "Jeff is still getting over a massive betrayal. For all we know he's just been saying those things about not wanting a relationship because he's scared to let anyone in and get hurt again."

"And what if you're wrong?" I said, picturing Jeff's smile, and thinking about the way he made me laugh. It almost made me want to say screw it, I'd take him any way I could have him, because the idea of not spending time with him made me feel hollow. But I knew in the end that if I gave in now, I'd only wind up feeling worse than I already did.

"You won't know unless you try."

I felt tears start to form in the corners of my eyes again. I wiped them away. "Ugh. I don't know what's wrong with me. I'm not usually this emotional."

"I know. This isn't like you at all. *You're* usually the pragmatic one, not the other way around." Jesse gave me a wary look. "Do not tell me you're pregnant."

I sat up like a bolt and glared at her. "That is so not funny."

She laughed. "Take it easy. I was just kidding."

Of course she was. And of course I wasn't pregnant, because I was smart and I used protection every single time I had sex. The last thing I needed on top of everything else was a baby.

"So, do you want to get out of here and do something?" Jesse asked, switching subjects seamlessly. "Or should we just rent a movie and stuff our faces with junk food?"

"Shouldn't you be with Justin celebrating your new job?"

"We can celebrate anytime."

"How about tagging along with me and Bailey on a walk?" I was in the mood for fresh air, hopeful it would help settle my still-queasy stomach, and walking my dog was always more fun when I had someone to talk to.

We didn't discuss Jeff. Instead I told her about how

crushingly awful my job interview that morning had gone.

"Now I feel like the most insensitive person on the planet," she said.

"No, don't. There's no way you could've known about it. And I really am happy for you."

"Something good is going to happen soon," she said. "You'll see."

I smiled, hoping she was right. I was long overdue for some good luck.

Before Jesse left I made her promise me something. "You won't tell Jeff what we talked about, will you?"

"Of course not. But sooner or later you're going to have to tell him why you ran out on him and why you won't answer his calls."

Whether or not I liked it, I knew Jesse was right. Jeff was part of my best friend's family. Even if I wanted to, there was no way I could avoid him forever.

Chapter 13
The Unexpected

I waited one more day before calling Jeff. By the time I dialed his number I still wasn't sure what to say even though I'd rehearsed the same speech in my head a thousand times.

"About the other night," I began as Jeff got on the phone. "I shouldn't have run off like I did."

"No. It was my fault. I probably said something I shouldn't have."

"You only spoke your mind," I said. "There's nothing wrong with that."

"I'm still not really sure how I pissed you off so badly."

"I wasn't really pissed," I explained. "I guess I just realized that this whole friends-with-benefits thing isn't for me."

"You could've told me that instead of taking off like you did." His voice sounded stiff. "Or called me the next day to explain instead of leaving me hanging."

"I didn't know what to say"

"Hmm. How about something like this: 'Jeff, I like you, and you're amazing in bed, but I prefer a platonic friendship.'"

I shook my head, trying not to laugh. If he was back to

making jokes I figured that meant he'd forgiven me. "Yeah, cause that's easy to tell someone."

"It's not easy to hear either. Talk about kicking my pride in the nuts, but it's better than having your dinner date run out of the restaurant without telling you why."

"I'm sorry," I said, realizing for the first time how confused and embarrassed he must have felt. "I've had a lot on my mind lately, and I wasn't really myself that night. I know that's not a good excuse, but I don't know what else to say."

"Is this because of your ex?" Jeff asked. "Are you still in love with him?"

His question totally took me by surprise. What had made him think that? "I can assure you I am not still in love with Greg."

"But you're not ready to be with someone else?"

"That's not really it, exactly," I said, trying to find the words to explain myself without confessing what the real problem was. "It's just that I don't think the two of us are looking for the same things. I know you don't believe in long-term relationships because of what happened with you and Nina, but despite everything, I still do."

Jeff sighed. "I hate leaving things like this."

"Does your offer of friendship still stand?"

"Of course."

"Then I'll take it."

Jeff grumbled. "I'm going to have to remember to take a cold shower before we see each other."

I laughed. If cold showers really worked, I'd need to start taking them myself. Seeing Jeff, knowing that we both wanted to rip each other's clothes off, but at the same time realizing that if we did I'd only wind up getting hurt after, was not going to be easy.

After I got off the phone, a part of me felt relieved that we'd talked, but I was also crushed that he hadn't told me I was wrong when I'd said that the two of us weren't looking for the same things. I really had hoped that somewhere along the line he'd changed his mind.

As the days passed, I waited for my somber mood to lift, but it only seemed to worsen. I wanted to blame it on the change of seasons, the cold weather, daylight savings time even, but those things happened every year and they'd never gotten me into the pit I was now in. I felt tired all the time and had to force myself to get out of bed in the mornings.

After tossing yet another bowl of half-eaten cereal in the trash, I remembered Jesse's joke about being pregnant. I knew I was being silly even considering it, but the more I thought about her words the harder it became to get that crazy 'what if' voice out of my head. I tried to remember the last time I'd had a period. My cycle was pretty irregular, so I never bothered to keep track of it. Maybe I'd had one in late September, or could it have been October?

What if Jesse was right and I really was pregnant? The thought began to drive me so crazy that I finally decided to stop at a drug store around the corner from my house. I brought the bag with the pregnancy test in it back to my apartment and set it down on my kitchen counter, telling myself I was silly for wasting fifteen bucks. Yet every time I tried to distract myself with something else it was like the box called to me, taunting me into thinking that maybe, just maybe, there was an explanation for the way I'd been feeling all week.

I broke down and brought the test into the bathroom with me, eager to get it done and ease the gnawing fear in my chest. There was no way I was pregnant, and in exactly two minutes I'd prove it to myself.

With shaky fingers, I unwrapped the test and sat down on the toilet. When I finished peeing I recapped the white plastic stick and set it down on my bathroom counter. It took only seconds for the result window to fill with a bright blue plus sign. My heart pounded in my chest. I literally felt like I was about to faint and had to hold on to the sink to make sure I didn't fall to the floor.

The test had to be wrong. I put my shoes back on and practically ran down the stairs on my way back to the drugstore. This time I picked the box with two tests in it. I brought it up to the cashier. She glanced at the box then back up at me.

"They're usually right the first time," she said.

I felt like telling her to mind her own goddamn business, but instead I just smiled and took the bag from her.

It turned out the cashier was right. The next two tests were just as positive as the first one.

I sat down on my couch and curled up into a ball. I didn't want to start crying again, but I couldn't help it. *How the hell had this happened?* I wasn't on the pill, because I'd tried them in the past and didn't like the way they made me feel, but I *always* insisted on condoms. They hadn't let me down a single time. What in the world had gone wrong? Anxiety flooded through my body, making me feel even sicker to my stomach than I had for the past week. I tried to slow my breathing, hoping it would calm me down.

Before I had a full-blown panic attack, I grabbed my keys and my bag. Bailey trotted over to the front door.

"Sorry, buddy," I said, scratching under his chin. Every time he saw me getting ready to go outside he got that 'take me with you' gleam in his eyes. "I promise I'll take you out on a long walk later."

I headed out and sprinted toward the train station and got on the first one that came, not really thinking about where I was going until I made it into the city. That's when I decided I desperately needed to talk to someone. A few stops later, I got off the train and headed to Jesse's building, praying she was home.

"Woah," she said after opening the door. I must have looked like the mess I felt. "What's wrong?"

Justin was sitting on the couch watching TV. He took one look at me after Jesse invited me in and asked, "Is everything okay?"

I nodded, afraid that if I spoke, tears would start spilling down my cheeks.

"Justin, honey. Do you mind giving me and Susan some time to talk?"

"Um. No. Of course not." Justin got up from the couch and walked over to us giving Jesse a quick kiss and me a pat on my shoulder before grabbing his keys and coat.

As soon as he closed the door behind himself, Jesse pulled me into the living room and sat me down beside her on the couch. "Tell me what's going on?"

I looked away, too mortified to meet her gaze. "I'm pregnant." The words just sort of tumbled out of my mouth. I waited for her to say something, but she just sat there silently. I tried to read her expression.

Jesse blinked a few times and then stared at me like I had snakes coming out of my mouth. "You're shitting me, right?"

"Why would I do that?" I said, wishing that I could've told her she was right. "Besides, you're the one who mentioned it the other day. If it wasn't for you I wouldn't have even thought about taking a pregnancy test, or two, or three."

"I was just kidding," she said, stretching her words for added drama. "Wait. You took three pregnancy tests and they were all positive?"

"Yup. I've got a row of plus signs all lined up on my bathroom counter."

Jesse leaned back, letting her back sink into the couch cushions. After another long stretch of silence she asked, "Did you tell Jeff yet?"

"No. I literally just found out, and when I did, I totally freaked, which is why I'm here. I need you to tell me what I'm supposed to do."

"You have to tell Jeff. He has a right to know he's going to be a father."

I swallowed the lump in my throat. "But what if he's not?"

"You're going to have an abortion?" Jesse asked, shocked that I'd even consider it.

"No." I shook my head. "I mean, I don't know, I haven't really decided what I'm going to do. What I was trying to say is that I don't know that the baby's Jeff's. It could be Greg's."

"Oh shit," Jesse muttered. "I didn't even think about that."

"How could this happen to me?" I said, feeling overwhelmed by my life. "I can't believe I'm pregnant and don't even know who the father of my baby is. I feel like such a slut."

"Stop that. You are not a slut. This could happen to anyone."

"I think I'm going to be sick," I said. A sudden wave of nausea rolled through my insides and I practically sprinted to the bathroom, just in time to throw up in the toilet. Jesse came up behind me and pulled my hair away from my face.

"Are you okay?"

I shook my head. "No, I'm not okay. I'm not okay at all," I said. "What am I going to do? I have no job, no health insurance, and I don't even know who the father of my baby is."

Jesse helped me off the floor, put her arm around my waist and led me back into the living room. "I think the first thing you need to do is make a doctor's appointment."

"How am I going to do that? I can barely afford rent and food." The more I thought about my situation the more I realized what an awful predicament I'd managed to get myself into. With a baby coming I'd need a job more than ever, and if I didn't find one soon I was going to be screwed. The chance of someone hiring me a few months from now when I'd be showing was next to zero. I'd been putting off getting a roommate because I kind of liked having the apartment to myself. I had an extra bedroom, but my apartment was still so small. With only one bathroom and nothing else but a tiny kitchen and living room, I'd be bumping into whoever shared that space with me all the time. Not that it even mattered now. Once the baby came, I'd need all the extra square footage I could get.

"How about this. You find the doctor, I'll take care of the rest," Jesse said.

I shook my head. "No way am I letting you pay my medical bills. I'll figure something out."

"You don't need any more stress. Just let me help you," Jesse said. "That baby you're carrying might very well be my niece."

I hadn't even thought about that. But niece or not, I didn't want to take Jesse's money. "What if it's not Jeff's?"

"Sue, you're like a sister to me. Even if Greg is the father, I'm still planning to be Aunt Jesse to your baby."

I had to keep myself from bawling at Jesse's words. I wondered if pregnancy hormones were what had me so emotional over the past couple of weeks. I remembered when my cousin Izzy had been pregnant, she used to cry every time a diaper commercial came on TV. Jesse's words touched me. I was an only child, which meant that my baby wouldn't have an aunt or an uncle, at least not on my side. Jesse offering to be one meant more than I could bring myself to tell her without starting another flood of tears.

"As long as you let me pay you back after I get a job and start making money." I didn't like the idea of borrowing money, but the only other person I could ask for help from was my mom, who would undoubtedly have a thousand questions about what I needed it for.

"I can go with you to the doctor if you want."

"You don't have to do that." I shook my head. "Besides, I'd rather not have my best friend there when the doctor does that whole legs-in-the-stirrups thing."

Jesse smirked. "Great. Now I'm not going to be able to get

that picture out of my head for the rest of the day."

"Jesse, you have to promise me something." I took both her hands and sandwiched them between mine. "You cannot say a word about this to Justin."

"Why not?"

"Because he'll tell Jeff, and I don't want him to know. At least not until I know who the father is."

"Fine. I promise. This is your secret to tell whenever you're ready. I swear I won't say anything to anyone."

Reassured, I leaned back, resting my head against the couch cushions and trying not to think about how I would break the news to either Greg or Jeff. I could already picture their reactions. Neither would be happy, I imagined. But like it or not, one of their lives was about to change big time, just like mine had.

Chapter 14
Thanksgiving

Talking to Jesse helped ease my anxiety, but as soon as I returned home I became riddled with fear all over again. I still couldn't really believe I was pregnant, but the tests that were lined up on my bathroom counter with their big blue plus signs practically glowing, were impossible to ignore, a reminder that there was a baby growing inside of me.

People were supposed to be elated when they found out they were going to have a child, but I was about as far from excited as a person could get. My life had veered so far off course over the past month I had no idea what to do with myself. And I was way too tired to try and figure it out, so instead, I went to bed.

Despite my somber mood I dragged myself out of bed the next morning and searched online for an OB in my neighborhood. The soonest doctor's appointment I could get was in two weeks. Before that, I had to make it through Thanksgiving at my mom's house. Normally I loved celebrating the holidays with her. She cooked way too much food—all of it delicious—and it was also a chance to see family I never got to for the rest of the year because we were all too busy with our lives. The prospect of a huge dinner while in the throes of morning sickness was not something I looked forward to, though. Unfortunately, bowing out was not an option.

Thanksgiving seemed to sneak up on me. I took Bailey for a long walk in the morning before changing out of my comfy yoga pants and into something fancy enough to earn my mother's approval. I hopped on the train headed to Bensonhurst with a bottle of red wine I wouldn't be able to drink in my hands.

My mother lived in a small duplex, the only house I'd ever known growing up. Now that I was on my own, I missed it. Not only was it way bigger than my apartment, but the neighborhood I grew up in felt like home in a way that Bay Ridge never did. Although as much as I missed it, I wasn't about to move back home with my mom the way a lot of kids I'd grown up with had. In high school my friends and I used to say we couldn't wait to get our own places. We all imagined this glamorous life in the city where we'd eat all our meals in fancy restaurants and then crawl into bed at two in the morning, drunk from yet another night out on the town. Then reality hit. No one I knew, including myself, could afford that kind of life. I made do with a small apartment in Brooklyn, but a lot of my friends gave up on paying New York rents altogether and moved back in with their parents. Of course, most of those friends had already gotten married and moved back out with spouses and now had a kid or two of their own.

I loved my mom way too much to mess up our relationship by cohabitating. For one thing, she was not an animal lover. She was also a total neat freak, the kind of person who covered her sofa with plastic until her child was old enough to know not to smear dirty handprints all over the upholstery.

The aroma of my mom's cooking greeted me as soon as I opened the door to her house. Garlic, tomatoes, basil. Normally, I loved those smells, but being pregnant had made scents I never even noticed before stomach-turning. I felt like I was going to be sick, but since I still hadn't told my mom about being pregnant, I didn't want to rouse her suspicions. If I ran into the bathroom to throw up, my mom would ask a thousand questions. I wasn't a very good liar, so I took small shallow breaths through my mouth instead of my nose.

"Susan, come into the kitchen," Mom called out as I shut the door behind me.

The smells only got worse closer to the kitchen. To distract myself, I tried thinking about other things, like the fact that I was about to meet my mother's boyfriend for the first time. As I entered the kitchen, Frank, who was seated at the table chopping sausage, put his knife down and got up to shake my hand.

My mom beamed as she introduced the two of us. Frank was on the short side, although taller than me and my mom. He had salt and pepper hair that was thinning in the front and steel blue eyes. Frank was not what I would have called handsome, but he seemed to have a warmth about him.

"It's so nice to meet you," Frank said. "Your mother talks about you all the time."

I knew that was something people usually said to be polite, but when it came to my mom I didn't doubt that it was true. I was her only child, after all. I still remembered when I first moved out on my own. She took it harder than I thought she would, but in the end, she realized Bensonhurst wasn't that far from Bay Ridge and stopped pleading for me to come back home.

"It's nice meeting you, too." I smiled and turned to my mom. "Do you need help with anything?"

"No," she said. "We're almost done." The doorbell rang, and she looked over her shoulder. "Actually, Susan, do you mind answering that?"

It was my mom's sister, Antonia, and her husband, Rick, who lived in Long Island. Thanksgiving and sometimes Christmas were about the only times of the year I saw them. My aunt and uncle had two children, but both of them were married now and only spent the holidays with us every few years, since they had in-laws to keep happy.

After a round of cheek-kissing and hugs, I helped them out of their coats and led them into the living room, where a girl I didn't recognize was seated on the couch.

My mom poked her head out of the kitchen. "Oh my," she said. "I almost forgot to introduce you to Frank's daughter."

I shook hands with her. She smiled and said, "I'm Stella. And you must be Susan."

"Yes. It's really nice to meet you."

Stella was a thin wisp of a woman with blonde hair that did not come from a bottle and blue eyes like her dad's. I was tempted to ask her what she thought of our parents dating, but I figured with them just in the other room, now was not the time for that conversation.

Antonia went to help my mom in the kitchen while Rick, Stella, and I set the table. A few minutes after we were done my mom came from the kitchen holding an enormous pan with a perfectly golden turkey. Turkey was about the only part of Thanksgiving at my mom's house that wasn't Italian. The rest of our meal consisted of pasta, braised greens, and roasted eggplant. Not your typical American Thanksgiving meal, but it was the food I'd grown up eating.

We all sat down except for Mom, who walked around the table filling glasses with the wine I'd brought. As she came over to where I was seated, I put my hand over my glass. "None for me."

She frowned. "I thought you liked merlot?"

"I do. I just don't feel like wine right now, that's all," I said, praying my refusal to drink wouldn't make her suspicious. I was probably being paranoid. Why would my mother think I was pregnant?

Thankfully, she didn't press the issue. After sitting down she invited Frank to say grace before starting our meal. As usual, her cooking amazed. I'd gotten used to the pungent smell of her Italian cooking, and my stomach managed to calm down enough that I was able to enjoy the meal.

Half-way through our meal Antonia chimed in with a question. "So Anna, how did you and Frank meet?"

I figured my mother probably didn't want her sister to know they'd met online so I cleared my throat and turned to my aunt. "Aunt Toni, can you pass the string beans?"

"Thank you," I said as she handed them to me. The moment's distraction gave the others at the table an opportunity to start talking about something else. Eventually the conversation drifted into a question-and-answer session for Frank, who didn't seem to mind talking about himself. I liked that he was friendly.

My mom needed someone like that, since she was such a social person herself. He launched into an abbreviated biography, telling us about being a retired police officer. He'd lost his wife a few years ago after a long battle with breast cancer. Stella was his baby, she lived in the city and worked as a network engineer for HBO. In addition to her, he also had two sons who lived in Jersey and were cops like he'd been.

My uncle Rick was addicted to cop shows and had a million questions for Frank, who seemed to like sharing his most gruesome and entertaining stories. This being New York, he had plenty of them to tell. I began to see why my mom was so taken with Frank. He had a commanding presence, but at the same time seemed really gentle.

After eating way too much food, Mom brought out dessert. Instead of pumpkin or apple pie, we had tiramisu. No one complained about breaking with tradition because my mom's tiramisu was way better than anything you could get from a five-star New York restaurant.

I was too tired to stay much longer after dessert. After helping my mom with the dishes I said my goodbyes, despite her insistence that it was still early.

As soon as I reached my apartment, she called. "Susan, honey, is everything all right? You seemed strange tonight."

"I'm fine," I said, hoping I sounded convincing. "I'm just tired. I stayed up way too late last night watching a movie."

"What did you think of Frank?" she asked.

I smiled. "He's nice, Mom, real nice. I'm glad you two found each other."

After getting off the phone, I settled down on the couch. My hand drifted down to my belly, which of course was still flat, but I couldn't help but think about the little baby growing inside me. A week ago, when I'd found out I was pregnant, the news had sent me into a tailspin. But somehow since then I'd gradually found myself feeling almost excited at the idea of being a mother, even if it meant raising a baby all by myself. I could be content with that. Just me and baby, and Bailey. That would be my new happily ever after.

Chapter 15
Dr. Lu

In the free time I had between substitute teaching and dog walking, I spent a lot of it in front of the computer, job hunting and reading everything I could about pregnancy. Despite unrelenting nausea, an almost constant desire to crawl back into bed, and fear about what the future held, every article I read only furthered my conviction that I wanted to keep the baby. Growing up Catholic meant hearing all the time about abortion being a mortal sin. For a few days after finding out I was pregnant, I seriously considered it, but in the end I decided it wasn't something I could do.

That didn't mean I stopped worrying about what having a baby would mean. I worried all the time about the day I'd have to tell Jeff or Greg he was about to be a father. I hadn't heard from Greg since the last time he'd texted, asking for my engagement ring back, and I hadn't heard from Jeff since I'd told him our friends with benefits arrangement wasn't what I wanted.

Then one afternoon my doorbell rang. A delivery, the man on the other end of the intercom said. I let him in and after climbing the two flights of stairs to my apartment, he handed me a giant bouquet of flowers.

Puzzled, I looked for a note and found it buried between two blood-red roses. I pulled the card out of the small envelope it came in and read.

I miss you, Sue.
When can we hang out again?
Jeff

The flowers were gorgeous, but I didn't know what to make of the note. Jeff was good with subtle innuendo. Was he trying to find his way back into my life so we could hook up again, or was he asking to hang out as friends?

I sighed and set the card on the kitchen table. As much as I missed Jeff's company, I refused to give in to my desire to see him. Especially now. Being pregnant changed everything. The baby wouldn't be here for a long time, but he or she had already become my priority. Even if the baby turned out to be Jeff's, he still was who he was, and I didn't believe in trying to change people.

I took the bouquet into my living room, placed it on the side table next to the couch and leaned forward to take in their scent, which was as lovely as the flowers were. Just then my phone rang.

"Is Susan Calabro available?" the woman on the other end of the phone asked.

"Yes, I'm Susan," I said. "Who's calling?"

"My name is Linda Coleman, and I'm an administrator at Promises Daycare in Park Slope. I was calling to ask if you're still interested in a job with us."

"Yes. Absolutely," I replied, even though it wasn't exactly the truth. I really had my heart set on working at an elementary school, but I didn't have the luxury of waiting for an opportunity like that to come up.

"Great. Then I'd like to set up a time to interview you."

After getting off the phone I did an actual happy dance. I didn't even have the job yet, but getting called for an interview was the first bit of good luck I'd had in a long time. I set it up for a few days after my first prenatal appointment.

On the day of my appointment with Dr. Lu, the obstetrician I'd chosen, I arrived early so I could fill out the required paperwork. I'd never in my life been so nervous about setting foot in a doctor's office. As I sat there waiting for my name to be called, it was impossible not to notice all the pregnant women seated beside their husbands or boyfriends. More and more women were having babies on their own these days I reminded myself, trying not to let myself feel upset that I was probably the only single mother-to-be in the waiting room.

The ten minutes it took before my name was called felt like forever. A medical assistant ushered me into an exam room where she checked my weight and blood pressure before leaving me to wait again. I flipped through a few magazines, but that did nothing to ease my nerves. I wasn't even sure what I was most anxious about, being pregnant in the first place or having to confide in my doctor that not only was I single, I wasn't even sure who the father of my baby was. I pictured the pitiful look Dr. Lu would give me when I explained my situation to her.

When she finally came in the room, her warm smile and friendly handshake instantly put me at ease.

"So," she said, flipping through the paperwork I'd filled out.

"I can see this is your first pregnancy, which means you probably have a lot of questions for me. Why don't we start with that?"

"Um, I guess the question I'm really wondering about is how and when to go about getting a paternity test," I said, wanting to get that part of my visit out of the way so I could stop worrying about how the doctor would react.

Dr. Lu leaned back in her chair. "You have a few options, but I'd have to know how far along you are in your pregnancy. Since you're not sure when your last period was, we'd need to do an ultrasound."

I nodded. "Okay."

"The ultrasound is performed transvaginally, so you'll need to remove your pants and underwear." She stood, retrieved a drape from the cabinet above her and handed it to me. "Let me give you some privacy to change."

If I was nervous before, now I was *really* nervous. Pelvic exams, ultrasounds, paternity tests, it was so much to take in, but it wasn't like I had a choice. After I took off my underwear and pants I sat down on the exam table with the drape covering my privates and took deep breaths to calm my nerves while I waited for Dr. Lu to return. When she did, she sat down beside me on a rolling stool.

"Are you doing all right?" she asked. "You seem awfully nervous."

"I guess you can probably tell this pregnancy wasn't what you would call planned."

"I figured as much. How do you feel about it, though? I mean besides being nervous? Are you happy?"

"I . . . I don't really know," I said, trying not to fidget. "I'm still not over the shock. I don't even know how this happened, because I always insist on condoms. I want to be a mother someday, just not like this. I was supposed to be married first, yet here I am, pregnant and single. I don't even have a boyfriend."

"Are you thinking about terminating the pregnancy?"

I shook my head. "No. I know I want this baby."

She put her hand on my arm. "You'll be surprised at how seemingly hopeless situations turn out well in the end."

I barely knew Dr. Lu, but I'd already dumped my plateful of problems on her lap and she'd found the exact right words to make me feel better. At least I'd picked the right doctor.

I lay down and Dr. Lu got started on my ultrasound. After a few minutes of manipulating the probe she pointed to the screen. "You see that there?"

At first, all I saw was grainy white shadows on a black background. I had no idea what I was looking at. Then I noticed something flashing back and forth on the screen. "What is that?" I asked.

"Baby's heartbeat."

"What?" I couldn't believe my eyes. A heartbeat. *My* baby's heartbeat. "You can see that already?"

"By the look of things, you're about eight weeks pregnant, so yes, we can definitely see a heartbeat now."

"Oh my God," I whispered. There was no way I was going to start bawling in front of my doctor, but I sure felt like I was about to. Seeing my baby's heartbeat hit me like a ton of bricks. There was a little boy or a little girl growing inside me, its heart was beating, it was making me sick and tired and an emotional mess, but I was already in love with him or her.

When Dr. Lu was finished she said, "Go ahead and get dressed and then I'll be back so we can talk some more."

In a trance, I pulled on my clothes. Dr. Lu came back in just as I finished buttoning my pants. "Questions?" she asked as she sat down.

"You said I was eight weeks pregnant." I was trying to mentally calculate what that meant in terms of the baby's paternity. "Does that mean I've been pregnant for almost two months?"

"We calculate how far along you are based on your last menstrual period. Typically that means your date of conception is two weeks after that, although none of these calculations are an exact science, not even with the ultrasound. It can be off by as much as a week."

Which meant I was no closer to figuring out who the father was. "What are my options as far as paternity testing goes?"

"At eight weeks you can get a DNA test done by having your blood drawn. We'd also need blood from one of the possible fathers. The other two pre-birth options are more invasive and carry a slight risk of miscarriage."

I shook my head. "I prefer the blood test then."

"The drawback to the blood test, unfortunately, is the price," she said. "It can cost well over a thousand dollars, and it isn't covered by insurance."

Ouch. That wasn't something I could afford. Jeff could, and maybe even Greg too, assuming they would be interested in paying for something like that now, instead of waiting until the baby was born, which I doubted, since neither of them would be in a rush to find out they were going to be a father.

"Or you can just wait until the baby is born," Dr. Lu said, reading my mind.

Hearing her suggest that as a possibility made the idea sound even better to me. Truthfully, it didn't really matter to me who the father was. I'd love my baby regardless.

"Can I have some time to think about it?"

"Of course. You don't need to decide anything today, but when you do, feel free to call the office and leave a message for me." Dr. Lu reached into a filing cabinet and handed me a folder filled with all types of pregnancy-related information. "I want you to read through this information before your next visit. It won't be for another four weeks, but if you have any questions before then, just call."

Once I got home, I scoured through the reading material from Dr. Lu's office, but it was hard to concentrate when all I could think about was that ultrasound. I couldn't get the picture of my baby's heartbeat out of my head. I laid the palm of my hand on my belly and looked down at my still flat abdomen. With me being thirty-two and still single, it was a distinct possibility that this would be my only child, which made me love him or her even more. I hadn't been lying when I'd told Dr. Lu I always wanted to have a baby. I loved children, it was the reason I'd decided to become a teacher. I adored their innocence and the way they loved unconditionally.

So, despite not having a real job, or health insurance, and with almost nothing in savings, one way or another, I intended to make things work for me and my baby.

Chapter 16
A Party

I was almost as nervous for my job interview as I had been for my doctor's appointment. As I got out of bed that morning I tried to ignore the voice in my head that told me I was wasting my time because there was no way I'd get offered the job.

As I showered I kept telling myself that it was time to get back to being my old self. The Susan who was confident, cheerful, and outgoing. This new Susan, who seemed to emerge after my love life had imploded and a surprise pregnancy had sent my hormones into overdrive, was an emotional train wreck, and I didn't like her.

I paired black dress pants with a silky blue blouse and headed out with my fingers crossed. The daycare center was in Park Slope, an affluent Brooklyn neighborhood, so it didn't take me long to get there.

As it turned out, the manager at Promises Daycare, Linda, was an animal lover, and when I'd told her about the years I'd spent as a vet tech and dog walker before getting my education degree, she seemed to take an immediate interest in me. At the end of the tour of the center, she offered me the job.

"It's contingent on passing a background check," she said. "Although I'm sure that won't be a problem."

"No, it won't be," I assured her. "Thank you so much. I just know I'll love it here."

So it wasn't my dream job, but the daycare center looked really nice and modern, and Linda seemed like she'd make a great boss. Another bonus was the easy commute. Elementary education had been my major, and while teaching a group of four-year-olds wasn't exactly the same as second or third grade at an elementary school, it wasn't that far off. I wouldn't be educating kids on addition or improving their writing skills, but Promises did have a curriculum for the preschool class, so I wouldn't just be babysitting, there would be some actual teaching involved. Besides, a job there meant a steady paycheck, and, best of all, health insurance.

"Okay. I'll be in touch as soon as all the paperwork is in order." Linda stuck her hand out. I shook it and thanked her profusely.

I called my mom first to share the news with her. She wanted to take me out to dinner to celebrate. Normally I would have said yes, but I still hadn't told her about the baby and was starting to feel guilty about keeping such a big secret from her. Sooner or later I'd work up the courage to tell her I was pregnant, but right now I just wanted to be excited about my new job and enjoy the calm before the storm.

I called Jesse after. "How was your OB appointment?" she asked.

"It went well. I really like my doctor. Next time we hang out I'll fill you in on all the details," I said. "But right now I have other news."

"Is everything okay?"

"Yup. You're not going to believe this, but I think I have a job. If everything goes well with the background check, I'll be working full-time in a couple of weeks."

Jesse let out a happy squeal. "Oh my God," she said. "I'm so excited for you. Where? Tell me!"

After I filled her in on the details she said, "This is such perfect timing. Justin's having a get-together Saturday at our place to celebrate my first official teaching job. I was calling to invite you. Now I can tell him to make it a party for the both of us."

"Um, I don't know," I said. "Is Jeff going to be there?"

"Probably. He is Justin's brother after all."

"Then I'm not so sure it's a good idea."

I wasn't ready to see Jeff. My feelings for him hadn't gone anywhere. More than once I'd had to talk myself out of picking up the phone and calling him. And now that I could possibly be carrying his child, seeing him would be even harder.

"Susan, seriously. He might wind up being the father of your baby. You can't avoid him forever."

"I know, I know." Just saying his name out loud had made my heart quicken. I could only imagine how I'd feel when I saw him again. I wondered if he was upset that I hadn't called to thank him for the flowers. I knew I should have, but I just couldn't bring myself to pick up the phone. He was my drug. If I didn't quit him cold turkey, there was a pretty big chance I'd wind up back in his bed. "I just don't think I can handle seeing him with some girl draped over his arm," I said, certain he'd already found some other girl to keep him busy.

"To tell you the truth, I haven't seen him with anyone since the two of you hooked up. And Justin keeps telling me that he thinks Jeff really likes you. If anyone would know, it's him."

I hadn't told Jesse about the flowers. They were starting to wilt, but I hated the idea of throwing them away. Even if she was right, and Jeff really did like me, the timing was all wrong. If it weren't for the baby, maybe I'd be willing to take a chance on him, but things were different now.

"I don't know, Jesse."

"Oh, come on, Susan, I really want you to be there," she said. She waited for my reply, but when I didn't give her one, she continued. "Please, you have to come. It's going to be fun, you'll see."

I didn't want to disappoint Jesse. "All right. I'll come," I said, hoping I didn't wind up regretting my decision.

The day before the party, I got a call from the daycare center telling me my background check was done and the job was officially mine. Linda gave me a projected start date. I got off the phone elated at the idea of not only a real teaching job with kids I got to see every day, but also a steady paycheck. I took the call as a good omen and decided to stop fretting about seeing Jeff for the first time in almost a month. My luck was turning, I could just feel it.

I was still so excited about my new job that the next day, while getting ready to go to Jesse's, I didn't let myself feel bothered that I could hardly find a pair of pants that fit me anymore. I wasn't really showing yet, but everything I tried on felt tight and uncomfortable. I had no choice but to wear leggings, which I paired with a long tunic-style top and knee high boots.

When I got to Jesse's apartment, she greeted me with a hug. Justin came up right behind her with two glasses of champagne, one of which he handed to me. I took that to mean that Jesse had kept her promise to not tell him about my pregnancy.

"You're right on time," Justin said. "Come on, let's toast you guys and your new jobs."

I followed them into the living room. They had a big apartment, but even with the large space and crowd of people, it took only a few seconds for me to spot Jeff standing near the sliding glass door that led out to the balcony. He was talking to Jesse's brother Mike. Even from across the room there was something magnetic about him and I had to fight the pull, the urge, to walk up to him and look into those magnificent blue eyes of his again.

Justin turned down the music. "Thank you all for coming," he said loudly. As heads turned in his direction, he continued speaking. "I appreciate everyone coming out to celebrate Jess and Susan's good news. The two of them are going to make awesome teachers." He raised his glass. "So congrats to you, Jess." He put his arm around her and turned to look at me. "And to you, Susan."

Everyone began clinking their glasses together and sipping their champagne. I managed to sneak into the kitchen, where I emptied my glass into the sink. The volume of music and voices turned up, and I knew I should go find some friends to talk to, but I was too afraid of bumping into Jeff, certain the minute we started talking he'd finally figure out why I'd been avoiding him.

What I really wanted to do was turn around and go home. Instead I took a few deep breaths, pulled my shoulders back, and made my way over to a small group of people I knew from classes we'd taken together.

"Congratulations, Susan" said Eesha, an Indian woman who'd been in some of my elementary education classes. She and I were about the same age. The university I'd graduated from had a pretty good mix of students. A lot were fresh out of high school, but a fair number were older like me and Eesha.

"Thanks." I managed a smile and stopped myself from confessing that my fabulous new job was actually teaching four-year-olds at a daycare.

"You and Jesse are so lucky," said Andrea, another former classmate. "I can't even count how many resumes I've sent out and I haven't gotten a single call."

The conversation quickly devolved into an all-out gripe fest about how bad the job market was for education majors. I managed to ease myself away and went back to the kitchen to look for something to eat.

"Hey Sue." Mel was also in the kitchen, fixing herself a plate.

I smiled at her. "How's it going?"

"Good." She gave me a strange look. "How come you don't look happy? This party is supposed to be for you."

"I've got a lot on my mind, that's all."

"You want to talk about it?"

I shrugged. It was nice of Mel to offer, but we weren't that close and I didn't want to say anything about Jeff since he was just in the other room. "No, not really" I said, trying not to sound like I wasn't grateful for her offer.

"Just don't let it be a guy that's got you down. They're not worth it," Mel said.

Just then Jesse walked into the kitchen. "Hi Mel," she said before turning to me. "I've been looking for you, Sue."

I could tell by the look in her eyes that whatever she wanted to tell me was better said in private. I left my plate on the counter and followed Jesse out of the kitchen and down to the end of the hallway where the bedrooms and bathroom were.

"I can't believe you haven't even said hi to Jeff," she said. "That's not cool."

"I just haven't had a chance to make my way over to that corner of the room, that's all."

"Susan, c'mon. You're already almost three months pregnant with a baby that could very well be his and you're pretending he doesn't even exist."

"That's not true," I insisted, even though she had a point. If the baby was Jeff's, I'd have to figure out a way to be around him.

Jesse raised her brows. "Seriously? This is me you're talking to."

"Okay, I got it. I'll go say hi."

I started to walk away, trying not to be pissed that Jesse couldn't just let me handle things the way I wanted to. She reached for my arm and I turned back around. "When are you planning on telling him that you're pregnant?" she asked.

"After the baby is born."

Jesse shook her head. "No. You cannot wait that long."

"Why not?"

"What are you going to tell him when you start showing?"

"I don't see him that often, so he doesn't need to find out now." I could tell she didn't like my answer, so I continued, "The prenatal paternity tests are either too expensive or too risky for the baby, so I decided to put off the DNA testing until after the baby's born," I said, "I'll tell Jeff and Greg about the baby then, even though truthfully, I don't really need to know which one of them is the father, I can raise this baby by myself. It's better this way. Neither of them wants to be a father."

"You don't know that!" Jesse said, incredulous.

"Can we not talk about this right now?" I glanced over my shoulder. "What if someone hears you?"

Jesse frowned. "Fine. But we're not done discussing this."

She walked away leaving me by myself. I took a deep sigh, trying to pull myself together before heading back toward the living room. I already felt bad enough without a lecture from Jesse. I couldn't believe how unsympathetic she was being. Trying to figure out what the right thing to do was hard enough, I didn't need her laying a guilt trip on me on top of everything else.

As I rounded the corner on my way back to the kitchen I bumped right into Jeff. With my eyes reddened from the tears I'd just fought back it was the exact worst time to run in to him.

"I'm sorry." My face flushed at the sight of him. "I wasn't looking where I was going."

"Um, yeah. I'm sorry, too. I was just on my way to the bathroom," he said, stuttering. He lifted his gaze to mine. "Are you okay?"

I nodded, feeling myself pale as I tried to breathe through a sudden bout of nausea. "I'm fine."

I should've said more than that. I should've asked how he was doing, but my brain froze, and I just couldn't come up with the right words even after I noticed the disappointment on Jeff's face. The last time we talked I'd agreed to be friends. No doubt the cold shoulder I'd been giving him had to be confusing. But why should he care? I was just one woman in a long line of them who he'd shared his bed with.

I walked away before Jeff had a chance to say anything else. The plate I'd filled with food earlier was still in the kitchen where I'd left it, but my appetite had vanished, along with my desire to socialize. I just wanted to go home and crawl under my covers and not think about paternity tests or Jeff, or anything else. Without saying good-by to anyone I retrieved my coat from Jesse's bedroom and snuck out of her apartment. I made my way down to the lobby, zipped up my coat, and walked outside into the frigid Manhattan air. Too deep in thought, I didn't notice Jeff trailing me on my way to the train station until I heard my name being called.

"You and I need to talk," he said, as he caught up to me.

I panicked, worried that he'd overheard my conversation with Jesse. What if he knew about the baby?

Chapter 17
A Confession

In contrast to Jeff's tone, I tried to keep mine light. There was no way he knew anything, I told myself. If he did, he would have already come right out with it. "Yeah, sure," I said, digging my hands into my coat pockets. "What do you want to talk about?"

"What's going on with you?" he said. "Why are you giving me the cold shoulder? Have I done something to piss you off?"

I shook my head. "I don't know what you're talking about. I'm not giving you the cold shoulder."

"You didn't even say hello to me up there," he said, gesturing toward Jesse's building. "And I know you got the flowers I sent. You could have at least texted me after you got them."

"Is that what this is about?" I snapped, even though I'd promised myself I wouldn't let my emotions get the best of me. "I didn't come running over to your place after you sent me flowers and a booty call note, so you're mad?"

"Booty call? Is that really what you thought? That I sent you flowers just to get you back in bed? Why would I do that after you told me that's not what you want?"

My cheeks heated. It was wrong of me to assume the flowers

came with ulterior motives. "Then why did you send them?" I asked in a calmer voice.

"It was like I said in the note. I missed you, and I wanted to see you." He stared down at his feet for a second before meeting my gaze again. "After our last conversation I couldn't stop thinking about you." Jeff took a step closer. "I like you, Sue. I wanted to tell you that sooner, but I was worried you were still hung up on your ex."

His words left me tongue-tied. "I . . . I'm not sure what you're trying to say here."

"I'm saying that I want us to get to know each other better. I want to take you out to dinner and the movies and see where this thing between us goes."

For a moment I didn't know how to respond. I hadn't expected to hear those words from him. "Whatever happened to "there's too many fish in the sea"?" I finally said.

Jeff looked right at me, his eyes meeting mine. "The only fish I'm interested in is you. But now I'm wondering if I read the situation between us all wrong," he said. "I suppose this is karma. The one girl I actually like, doesn't like me back."

I took a few slow, deep breaths. I knew I'd heard Jeff right, but I just couldn't bring myself to believe he was being sincere. "For how long? A few weeks? You said it yourself, you don't believe in true love, *or* long-term relationships."

"I was being stupid when I said that to you," he said, running a hand through his hair. "There was a time I believed in both of those things, and then . . . well, I told you what happened. But I don't know, lately I've been thinking that this new Jeff isn't me. Because if it was I wouldn't be missing you the way I do. I wouldn't be checking my phone a hundred times a day to see if you'd called, and I wouldn't feel so damn miserable that you can't even manage to say hi to me at a party."

He inched closer to me. Too close. I wanted to grab him and plant my lips on his. He reached for my hand and my heart started doing crazy backflips.

"I really like you, Susan, and maybe I'm an idiot, but I thought the feeling was mutual. You said you were over Greg, so why won't you give me a chance?"

I looked away, unable to meet his gaze. He was saying all the right things, things only a few weeks ago I wanted so badly to hear, but our circumstances had changed. "I do like you. I'm just not ready to take a chance. Not after what happened with Greg and the way he left me. I can't go through something like that again."

He let go of my hand and took a step back. "I'm not Greg."

"You just don't get it," I said, shaking my head.

"What don't I get? You're not really telling me anything that makes sense. Have you met someone else? Is that what this is about? Am I just too late? Because if that's the case, tell me, so I won't keep trying to figure out what the hell is wrong with me that you won't even give me a chance."

Hot tears started to trail their way down my cold cheeks. Jeff's words had me aching for him. I desperately wanted to be in his arms and feel his lips on mine. I wanted what he wanted—to go out to dinner and the movies and get to know each other better. I could picture myself falling in love with him one day, and practically feel the joy that came along with it. But once I told him about the baby, everything would come to a screeching halt.

My heart couldn't bear that. "You don't want to know. You think you do, but you're wrong."

"Don't I get to be the judge of that?" Jeff took my hand again. His was warm, unlike mine. It was already December and the frigid air had begun seeping its way under my coat. "Just tell me."

I lifted my head and stared straight into his eyes. The city lights made it bright enough that I knew he could see my tears. "You want to know why I can't go out with you?" Jeff nodded. Bracing myself for his reaction, I continued, "Fine, then I'll tell you. I'm pregnant, Jeff. That's why."

He looked at me like a deer caught in someone's headlights. "You're . . . pregnant?"

I nodded and squeaked out, "Yes."

"How long have you known?"

"A few weeks."

"So I'm going to be a father and you're just telling me now?"

"Jeff, the baby might not even be yours," I said. Forcing those words out was painful, like ripping off a Band-Aid. "It could be Greg's."

The look on Jeff's face—a mix of shock and confusion—made me wish I hadn't just blurted out the news. "I . . . I don't know what to say."

"There's nothing to say. After the baby is born, we can get a paternity test done. That gives you another six months to decide whether or not you want to be a father, just in case the baby is yours."

Jeff just stared at me. I wanted to shout at him, to tell him to say something, anything that would make me feel like he was even the slightest bit excited at the prospect of fatherhood. But I couldn't force him to feel that way, or blame him either. I took a step away from him and wrapped my arms around my body, trying to warm myself up while he stood there in a state of shock. At least now he knew. I'd gotten telling him about the baby over with. Out of the corner of my eye, I saw a cab approaching and ran to the curb to hail it.

Jeff called out to me. "Sue, wait. We're not done talking."

I ignored him. As the cab door opened, his hand latched onto my arm. I glanced at him before shaking my arm free. "Yes," I said. "We are."

I got inside the taxi and slammed the door shut. After giving the driver instructions on how to get to my apartment I unleashed the torrent of tears that I'd done my best to hold at bay in front of Jeff.

Before I knew it, the cab driver had pulled up to the curb in front of my building. I paid him before running upstairs and straight toward the comfort of my warm bed, wishing that this day had never happened.

Chapter 18
More Flowers

I woke up the next morning with a sick feeling in my stomach, although this time it had nothing to do with the baby. No matter how hard I tried, I couldn't get Jeff's shocked expression out of my mind. Not that I could blame him. But I had at least hoped for a few words of encouragement—especially after he'd shared that he had feelings for me—something along the lines of 'if the baby is mine, I'll help any way I can.' Obviously a baby was the last thing he wanted, and even though I suspected he'd feel that way, it hurt like hell that he'd confirmed it.

I scooted over to the side of my bed that was pressed against the wall and pulled the curtains back to let in some light, but instead of sun a light drizzle fell. The gray day matched my dark mood. As cold as it had been over the past few days I was hoping for snow, not rain. The only thing worse than walking dogs in wet weather was walking dogs in *cold*, wet weather.

I pulled myself out of bed and headed into the kitchen where I made myself a steaming cup of herbal tea, hoping it would chase away the chill I felt inside. Bailey walked over and plopped himself right at my feet as if he knew I needed cheering up. As I stroked the top of his head, he looked up at me, with his tail wagging—an instant pick-me-up.

As I sat there drinking my tea Jeff's name illuminated the screen of my phone. I wasn't up for another conversation about the baby, so I let the call go to voicemail. The phone rang again, and then again. Then a text came in.

Please answer or I'll just keep calling until you do.

Why couldn't he just take a clue and realize that the reason I wasn't picking up was because I wasn't ready to talk? When he called back again, I almost ignored my phone before deciding at the last minute to answer.

As soon as I mumbled hello he said, "The only reason I keep calling is because I have something I need to tell you. Something important."

"I know that at some point we have to talk about the baby," I said. "But I'm just not ready to right now."

"I get it, but you can't just tell me that I'm going to be a father and expect me to sit around waiting for you to be ready to discuss it. That's not really fair."

I thought I'd made it clear that I wasn't sure who the father of my baby was. Maybe he'd been so shocked by news that he'd blanked on that part of our conversation. "Like I told you last night, the baby might not even be yours."

"That's actually the reason I called."

"What is?" I asked, wondering what he was getting at.

"You said last night you weren't sure if the baby you're carrying is mine or Greg's, but I am. I know who the father is."

"Really? How? Are you some kind of DNA psychic?"

"The baby is mine," Jeff said, ignoring my sarcastic remark. "I know it."

My insides twisted. "You know this how?"

A long pause followed. "That night when we had sex for the first time, something happened. Something I should have told you about before."

"What do you mean?" I asked, feeling frustrated and confused at the same time. Whatever Jeff was trying to say I wanted him to just spit it out already.

"The condom I used broke," Jeff said. "I know I should have said something then, but I was still partly drunk and caught up in the moment. I just didn't think it was a big deal. I figured I'd tell you in the morning, but then when I woke up, you were gone, and I was so busy wondering if I'd said or done something to make you leave that I forgot all about the stupid condom."

His confession should have made me furious, but I'd long gotten over the shock of being pregnant, and there was no undoing it. "Jeff, that doesn't prove anything" I said, refusing to get my hopes up that he was right.

"You don't get it. I know I'm the father. I can feel it. Maybe you don't believe in intuition, but I do."

"Intuition is not proof, Jeff." A broken condom certainly did increase the probability that the baby was Jeff's, but it wasn't a certainty. Only a DNA test could determine beyond a shadow of a doubt who the father of my baby was.

"Then we get proof, but until you can show me a test that says I'm not the father I intend to be the best dad in the world, and that starts with me going with you to your doctor appointments, and bringing you ice cream in the middle of the night when you're craving it."

I wasn't sure what to say. I hadn't expected him to tell me any of the things he just had. His offer to be there for me and the baby was beyond tempting, but I needed to think about more than just what I wanted. I had to think about what was going to be right for me and my child in the long run. "It's great that you're trying to be a good guy about this whole surprise pregnancy of mine, but it's really not necessary. I just got a job, which means health insurance and a regular paycheck. I can do this. I can raise a baby on my own."

"What are you saying? That you don't want me around?"

"What I'm saying is that I appreciate you wanting to be there for me and the baby, but I don't need your help." As the words left my mouth I realized they sounded harsh, which wasn't what I was trying to be, but I couldn't let myself believe in illusions. I wouldn't open up to Jeff only to have him realize that being a parent or dating someone so much older than he was, wasn't actually what he wanted. Although none of those things would matter if Jeff turned out to be wrong about being the father, since there was still a chance that Greg was.

"A baby needs a dad," he said in a firm voice.

"What if you wind up being wrong, and Greg is really the father? I don't want you to start getting attached to a baby that might not even be yours."

"Greg is not the father," Jeff said, cutting me off. He sounded upset that I'd even suggested the possibility. "Just answer one question for me. When is your next doctor's appointment?"

"In another three weeks. Right after Christmas."

"I'd like to come."

"I . . . I don't know, Jeff."

"Why are you doing this, Susan? Why are you pushing me away?"

Because letting him get close was only asking for trouble. But I couldn't tell him that. "That's not what I'm trying to do." It wasn't my intention to push him away, I was only trying to protect my heart.

"You know what. I'm not going to pressure you into anything. Just think about what I said last night. I like you, and I want to be with you. The fact that you're pregnant doesn't change that. Give me some time to show you that I mean it. And if you're still not convinced, or if I'm not what you want, I'll let you go."

There was so much passion in Jeff's voice that I just couldn't bring myself to ignore the flicker of hope that blossomed inside of me. Despite my nagging fear, he'd made it impossible for me to come right out and say no. "Fine," I said. "I'll think about it."

Flowers arrived at my apartment the next day, and then the day after that. By the end of the week my apartment was filled with so many bouquets, my living room looked like a floral shop. All week I went back and forth in my mind, telling myself to take Jeff at his word, but then later worrying he couldn't possibly mean what he'd said about wanting me and the baby not changing that.

Anxious for a distraction and some advice, I called Jesse. We decided to meet later at the bar downstairs for appetizers. I arrived first and ordered Buffalo wings to feed the serious craving for spicy food I'd recently developed.

As I sat waiting for Jesse, Donna spotted me and came over. "Please tell me you're meeting that delicious guy you came in here with a few weeks ago."

I shook my head. "No. I'm waiting for Jesse."

"What was his name again?" she asked. Donna tended to have a one-track mind when it came to good-looking men. She was the type that would rather date the handsomest asshole on the planet than a sweet, but less-than-gorgeous, guy.

"You mean Jeff?"

"Yeah, that was it. How could I have forgotten?" she said, smiling. "I heard about you and Greg. Looks like you've traded up."

"Jeff is not my boyfriend. We're just friends."

"What? Why didn't you tell me that before? If I would've known you two weren't dating I would totally have given him my number."

I tried not to let her words bother me, even though I knew that next to Donna I was downright plain. Regardless of how cold it was, she always wore clothes that showed off her tiny waist and surgically enhanced breasts. Donna was the kind of woman who turned heads wherever she went. But she hadn't seemed to turn Jeff's. I remembered being impressed that he hadn't seemed to take an interest in Donna at all.

Before I could think of a response I spotted Jesse as she walked inside. I quickly waved her over.

"Hey, Donna," Jesse said as she took off her coat and hung it on the back of her chair.

"Long time, no see," Donna said. "I hear congratulations are in order. Last time I saw you, you were still a single woman."

"Thank you," Jesse replied.

"I got to get back behind the bar," Donna said. "Do you guys want me to get any drinks started for you?"

"I'll have a mojito," Jesse told her.

"Just a Sprite," I said, managing a smile.

A few minutes later after our server brought our drinks over to the table I sighed and told Jesse, "I'm so jealous. It's not fair that when I need a drink the most I can't have one."

"There's always Ben and Jerry's," she said with a smirk on her face.

I groaned. "Why is everyone always offering me ice cream?"

"Everyone?"

"Okay, maybe not everyone." I paused. "Just you . . . and Jeff."

Jesse's eyes widened. "Start talking."

I told Jesse about my conversation with Jeff after the party and how I'd blurted out the news about being pregnant. Then I explained how he'd called me the following day insisting that not only was he certain that he was the father of my child but that he wanted to come with me to my prenatal appointments and bring me ice cream when the craving hit.

"Oh my God, that's so sweet," Jesse said.

"It is, I know. But I don't want to get my hopes up. If it turns out he's not the father, he's not going to want to take care of a baby that isn't his," I said, putting my biggest fear into words.

Jesse took a sip of her drink and reached for a buffalo wing. "You don't know that for sure. Instead of deciding for him, you should be happy that he wants to be a dad. That's awesome."

"I know it is. But I'm just scared that he's going to change his mind," I said. "What's going to happen when I get stretch marks or when I'm as big as a house? He's only twenty-four, he's gorgeous, and he's rich. Jeff can have any girl he wants. He's not going to want me."

Jesse shook her head. "Jeff's not like that."

"Weren't you the one who told me he was a player in the first place?"

"He was, but like I told you last week, I haven't seen him with anyone ever since the two of you hooked up. And when he was with Nina, he never even *looked* at another girl," Jesse said. "Besides, those women Jeff was screwing around with knew he wasn't interested in anything serious. He never lied to any of them. And he won't lie to you either. That's not who he is."

"Just because he won't lie to me doesn't mean he won't change his mind," I said, wiping sticky buffalo wing sauce from my fingers with a paper napkin.

Jesse frowned. "You remind me of Justin sometimes. I still remember when I asked him out and he came up with every reason under the sun why we shouldn't be together, even though he had feelings for me just like you do for Jeff."

"It's not the same," I said.

"Maybe not exactly, but that doesn't change the fact that both you and Justin are stubborn." She smiled. "No wonder I love the two of you so much."

I scowled at her and shoved another too-spicy buffalo wing in my mouth before gulping down the rest of my soda. Jesse just sat there laughing.

We polished off a second basket of wings, and then went upstairs to my apartment. After Jesse followed me inside, she stopped in her tracks once she noticed the flower arrangements sitting atop every formerly empty surface.

"They're from Jeff, aren't they?" she said.

"Yes."

Jesse shook her head and wandered over to a vase filled with colorful dahlias. "And you still think he's not interested?"

"He just wants me to let him come along to my next OB appointment."

"Then stop being so stubborn. Pick up the phone and call him," Jesse said. "Let him be there for you."

This was partly the reason I'd asked Jesse over. Because I just needed one last shove in Jeff's direction and I knew she'd give it to me. "Fine, fine. I'll call him. But not until you leave. You're going to make me nervous."

A smile spread across her face. She was clearly relishing her role as matchmaker. But I worried that if things didn't work out, Jesse would be torn between loyalty to her brother-in-law and loyalty to her best friend.

Later, after Jesse left, I sat on the couch staring at my cell phone, trying to work up the courage to dial Jeff's number. Instead I dialed my mom's.

"I was just about to call you," she said. "You're still coming on Christmas, right?"

My mom had long ago stopped trying to convince me to accompany her to midnight Mass, but Christmas day was another story altogether. I hadn't missed spending it with her even once since I'd left home. "Yeah, of course I'll be there."

"Perfect. Frank and his daughter will be here again. I hope it's okay if I don't invite anyone else. I think a small, intimate gathering will be nice for a change."

"Sure, Mom. That sounds nice."

Usually Christmas at my mom's house was a big production. She invited so much family, there weren't enough seats at the table, and I would have to go bring up a few extra folding chairs from the basement. I loved the chaos and noise, but it was a lot of work for my mom, and she wound up spending most of Christmas in the kitchen. I couldn't blame her for wanting to scale back. Besides, with only the four of us, this Christmas would be a lot easier on my wallet. It was only two weeks away and I hadn't even started shopping yet.

After I hung up, I stared at my phone, trying to work up the courage to call Jeff. For some reason I was almost certain he wouldn't answer, so when he came on the line it took me a moment to string words together.

"If you're still sure you want to come with me to my next doctor's appointment, then my answer is yes. I'd like you to come," I told him.

"Of course I'm still sure," he said. "In fact, I've never been more sure of anything."

"Okay, then I'll meet you there." I gave Jeff the address to my OB's office, along with the date and time of my next appointment.

"Can I see you before then?"

"Um, I guess."

"I'm leaving tomorrow for a business trip, but what about next weekend?"

"That's Christmas. I'll be at my mom's."

"How about some time during the week then?"

"I don't know," I said. "I start my job on Monday, and I'm not really sure what my schedule will be like."

"I really wish I didn't have to go on this stupid trip." He sounded disappointed.

"It's okay, Jeff. My appointment is in another two weeks.

We'll see each other then."

He let out a deep breath. "Okay. I guess I can wait."

"Jeff," I said, hoping to catch him before he hung up. "Thank you for the flowers; they're really beautiful."

"I'm glad you liked them."

Another delivery came the next morning. I figured they would have stopped once I agreed to let Jeff come with me to the doctor. As much as I loved all the bouquets, if he kept sending them I was going to run out of room in my apartment.

On Monday I started my job at Promises Daycare Center and Preschool. Linda introduced me to the rest of the staff and my classroom of children, who greeted me with a chorus of, "Good morning, Miss Susan." I fell instantly in love with their bright, happy faces and couldn't help but think that maybe I was meant to be a preschool teacher, after all.

The teacher I was replacing, Megan, guided me through the daily routines, which included teaching kids their letters and how to write their names, regularly scheduled potty breaks, recess, nap time, and lunch. It was a lot to remember, so I was grateful that Megan would be around for another two weeks to help with the transition.

"Honestly, the hardest thing about this job isn't the kids, it's their parents. They're all convinced their children are angels, whether it's true or not," she said. "But for the most part these are all good kids, which is why I don't want to abandon them before Christmas." She grinned. "And, I hate to admit this, but we get some awesome holiday gifts from their parents."

Megan wasn't exaggerating. By Friday, I'd only been working at Promises for a week but I still came home with a treasure trove of Starbucks gift cards, boxes of chocolate, and bath products.

Christmas snuck up on me. I'd managed to get a gift for my mom and Frank and even his daughter, Stella, but I didn't feel up for the usual festivities. I loved Christmas at my mom's, but between the gnawing voice in my head that kept asking when I was going to tell her about the baby, and worrying about the doctor's appointment I had in a few days, it was hard to get into a celebratory mood.

Mom outdid herself, perhaps because she had a smaller guest list this year. The first course was tortellini soup, which was followed by roasted lamb and potatoes, served alongside green beans, and homemade rolls. My mouth watered as I sat down at the table. Just like I'd read would happen in the packet of papers Dr. Lu had given me, my nausea had begun to subside. I was almost into my second trimester of pregnancy and grateful that my stomach had finally started to settle.

Mom had Frank say grace before starting our meal. When we were done eating, the four of us gathered in the living room. Just like every year, gifts were piled under the Christmas tree and my mom's antique nativity scene was set up in front of the fireplace, but I couldn't help but think that despite the familiar trappings, this Christmas was different. My mom had Frank, Greg and I weren't together any more, and biggest of all, I had a baby growing inside me.

Chapter 19
Test Time

A few days after Christmas, I had my second appointment with Dr. Lu. Knowing Jeff would be there had my stomach twisted into knots. I was just as nervous as I'd been the first time I'd stepped into her office.

By the time I arrived, he was already seated in the waiting room. He leapt up and rushed over as I pushed open the door, taking my hand.

"I'm pregnant, not disabled," I whispered to him. My nerves had me on edge.

"You're going to have to get used to me helping you," he whispered back.

After checking in, it only took a few minutes before the two of us were ushered into an exam room. The medical assistant took my blood pressure before handing me a gown and telling me to undress.

"Undress? For what?"

"You'll need a Pap smear today," she said.

She walked out of the exam room and closed the door behind her without giving me a chance to protest.

I glanced at Jeff. "You cannot be in here."

"Why not? You act like I haven't seen every part of you before." Jeff smiled at me devilishly, and my face heated.

"This is different. We're in a doctor's office."

"What if I promise not to look?"

Before I could answer, there was a tap on the door and Dr. Lu walked in. "Oops, I'm sorry. I thought you were already in the gown. I'll give you another minute."

Another minute was not enough time to both argue with Jeff and get changed, so I let him stay. I made him turn his head while I took all my clothes off and put that horrible monstrosity they called a gown on.

As promised, Dr. Lu returned a minute later. "So who do we have here?" she asked, looking at Jeff.

"Um, this is my friend Jeff. Jeff, Dr. Lu."

Jeff stood and shook her hand. "Susan and I are a bit more than friends, actually. I'm the baby's father," he said, sounding proud and confident at the same time. "That's why I'm here today."

Dr. Lu looked confused. She rifled through her paperwork. "Did you do the DNA test already? I thought you were going to wait until after the baby was born."

"Wait. There's a DNA test we can do now?" Jeff asked.

"Yes, absolutely," Dr. Lu said before realization took hold. She looked back and forth between us. "I get the feeling I'm missing something," she finally said.

Jeff glared at me, demanding an explanation.

"I didn't tell you about the blood test because it's too expensive," I said to him. "I can't afford it right now."

Jeff turned to Dr. Lu. "Well, I can."

"I would need Susan's consent since it requires a sample of her blood."

"I hate needles," I mumbled, looking away.

"You're due for a full panel of tests today anyway," Dr. Lu said.

I wanted to say no. I wasn't ready for everything that was happening. It was all too fast, but deep down I knew it was better to have my answer sooner rather than later. "Okay," I said, my voice weak. "I guess we can just add the DNA test on to the rest of them." I felt like throwing up. I thought I was done with morning sickness, but I was not prepared for the possibility that I'd have to call Greg and tell him he was about to be a father, or the look on Jeff's face when I told him he'd been wrong to assume he was. The idea made me feel ill. It was beyond crazy, but he actually seemed excited at the prospect of fatherhood, and I liked the way that made me feel. I didn't want to give it up.

"We'll need blood from you, too," Dr. Lu said to Jeff.

"That's not a problem," Jeff replied.

"Let's get started with your exam first," Dr. Lu said, turning her attention back to me. "Why don't you go ahead and lie down?"

I did as she asked, grimacing through the Pap smear and then barely listening as she explained about all the blood tests I was about to have done.

When everything was finally finished, Jeff and I walked outside together. He was quiet, and by the look on his face, still upset with me.

"I can't believe you're this mad about the DNA test," I finally said.

He spun around to face me. "Why didn't you tell me?"

"Didn't I already explain inside?"

"You mean that bullshit about the test costing too much? Did you really expect me to believe that, when you know I have more than enough money to pay for it?"

"I didn't want to have to ask you for the money," I said, trying to control my emotions. "You act like this is easy for me. Well, I have news for you, it's not."

"All the more reason to let me help you, but instead you keep pushing me away. Why?"

Snowflakes had begun to fall, dotting the sidewalk briefly before melting, leaving nothing but wet spots behind. They left the same drops of moisture on Jeff's cheeks and I had to stop myself from reaching out and wiping them away with my fingertips.

"Because I'm scared," I said a little louder than intended. "What if Greg is the father?" It was a possibility I didn't even want to think about. "I don't want that woman he left me for anywhere near my baby. Or what if you're the father and then you change your mind about wanting to be a part of this?"

"Do you really think I'm the kind of guy that would walk away from his own child? Because if you do, then I'm sorry I gave you that impression. I know I said some stupid things when we first met; but that's all it was, just talk, because I was afraid of getting hurt again. If I could take my words back, I would."

"This pregnancy wasn't exactly planned you know. I'm still trying to sort everything out," I said, trying my best to give in a little. Something I was remarkably bad at doing.

"We can sort things out together. But only if you let me in."

I looked up and stared into Jeff's impossibly blue eyes. They'd gone from angry and accusatory to soft and pleading. "What is it that you want from me, exactly?" I asked.

"I already told you that night after the party at Jesse's. I want to take you to dinner and to the movies. I want us to get to know each other better."

"And then what? What if you decide I'm not the person you want?"

"There are always going to be what-ifs, Susan. I've been lying in bed every night since the first one we spent together wondering about them. I'm just as afraid as you are of getting hurt and getting left behind—again."

"And if this baby isn't yours?" I said, resting my hands on my belly.

Jeff inched closer and reached out to lift my chin with his hand. "That's my baby. I already told you that more than once."

I looked away, too filled with fear to meet his gaze. He dropped his hand from my chin.

"I just need a little time to think things through," I said.

"Will you call me when the DNA results come in?" Jeff asked, taking a step back from me.

Ugh. Those damn DNA test results were going to be the only thing I'd be able to think about for the next few days until they were ready. I nodded. "Of course."

Jeff leaned in to give me a kiss on the cheek. "Thanks for letting me come today," he said before turning around.

I watched him walk away before heading in the opposite direction toward the train station.

Getting through the rest of the afternoon was an almost

impossible task. My new boss had agreed to let me come in late after I explained that I'd set up a doctor's appointment weeks ago, but I almost regretted not just calling in sick and taking the entire day for myself. Not that that would've been any better. At least the kids distracted me enough that I managed to muddle my way through the rest of the day.

On the train ride home I replayed my conversation with Jeff over and over in my head. I kept telling myself I should be thrilled at what he was offering. A real relationship. And he seemed genuinely happy about the baby. But that could all change with one blood test result. Every time I raised the possibility of the baby being Greg's, Jeff just insisted I was wrong, but not once had he told me how he'd feel and what he'd do if Greg was the father.

The next few days were the longest of my life. I was wound tighter than a spool of thread. Falling asleep was a chore. I had no appetite, and no desire to talk to anyone. I spent New Year's Eve alone, huddled on my couch with the TV on, watching other people celebrating.

Work became a welcome distraction, but as soon as I clocked out for the day my thoughts turned to Jeff and the DNA results. Every evening, as soon as I got home I turned the ringer off on my phone and sat on the couch in front of the TV until I finally drifted off to sleep.

And then, a week after I'd gotten my blood drawn, just as I was bundling up to head home after work, I got a call from Dr. Lu. As soon as I saw her number displayed on my phone I knew why she was calling. My heart started thumping so hard, for a second I almost felt like I was going to pass out.

"I have your DNA results," she said.

I sucked in a breath and held it for a moment. "Yes?" I managed to choke out.

"Your handsome friend was right. He is the father of your child."

My heart felt like it went from racing a mile a minute to almost stopping. I had to remind myself to breathe. "You're absolutely sure?"

"Yes. Absolutely."

"Oh my God, Dr. Lu," I said, feeling tears start to work their way down my cheeks. "Thank you *so* much."

"It's a weight off your shoulders, knowing, isn't it?"

She was right. For the first time since I'd found out I was pregnant, I felt like I wasn't drowning in worry. Everything I'd been so anxious about seemed to fade away. After wiping my eyes and forcing my hands to stop shaking, I dialed Jeff's number, almost not caring if something might have changed since the last time I'd seen him. I could handle that a lot better than I could co-parenting with Greg.

"So I guess you knew what you were talking about," I said as soon as he answered.

"What do you mean?"

"Dr. Lu just called. The DNA tests are in and you were right."

"I . . . I'm going to be a dad?"

I smiled. "Pretty much."

Jeff whooped like a frat boy on his first spring break. "I knew it. I knew it, I knew it," he said. "Where are you right now?"

"At work. I was just about to leave when Dr. Lu called."

"Can you wait for me to get there? I need to celebrate and I'm not doing it without you."

"Jeff, I . . ."

"C'mon, Sue. Give a guy a break. It's not every day you find out you're about to be a father. Let me enjoy this."

His joy was infectious and I found myself smiling wider than I had in a long time. "Okay. I'll wait for you in the staff lounge."

I practically jumped out of my chair when he arrived. Jeff walked over to me with a broad smile on his face, and I couldn't help but return it as he wrapped his arms around me.

"What are you in the mood to eat?" he asked. "I want to take you out for dinner."

I'd been having the most insatiable craving for red meat over the past few days. "How about some Korean barbecue?" I said, looking up at him.

He smiled. "I know the perfect place."

I followed him outside and we got into the cab that had been waiting for him. Jeff gave the driver an address, and the man took us to a small restaurant that was packed with people. I was sure we'd have to wait forever for a table, but the hostess took us to a table for two tucked away in the corner. Since I couldn't drink alcohol, Jeff asked for two glasses of water and we toasted with that instead of wine.

"To us," Jeff said as we lifted our glasses.

"To us," I repeated.

Jeff took a sip of his water and then placed it down on the table in front of him. "You know what I just realized? This is pretty much our first real date."

"No. We've been out to dinner before."

"Oh, you mean the time you ran out on me," he said, teasing. "I've been trying to block that night from my memory."

"I'm sorry. The last thing I wanted was to make you feel bad. I should have told you what was in my head instead of running off," I said. "But to be fair, it's not just a myth; pregnancy hormones can make a girl a bit crazy."

"It's okay." Jeff took another sip of his water. "I mean at first I felt like a total loser, but then after you explained, I understood. I'm just glad we've moved past that. Past me making an ass of myself by pretending you weren't as special to me as you are, and past me over-thinking how crazy this whole thing between us is."

"Crazy? You mean because of the baby?"

Jeff shook his head. "No. I'm talking about the way I feel when it comes to you. When you really think about it, we barely know each other. We've only hung out a few times, but I like you . . . a lot. More than I've liked anyone in a long time."

"I like you a lot, too," I said, ignoring the voice in my head that kept saying I was insane for being this open, for letting him in so soon and not waiting until he proved to me that I could trust him with my heart.

Before Jeff could respond, the waitress came by with our dinner orders. The smell of all the spices and seasoning made my mouth water. I stabbed a piece of meat with my fork and shoved it in my mouth, savoring my first bite of food since lunch.

After we finished eating, Jeff took care of the check, and the two of us stepped back outside into the frigid air. Jeff reached for my hand. "You think I can convince you to come to my place so we can talk?"

I arched an eyebrow. "Just talk?"

"Yeah. Just talk," Jeff said. "Believe it or not I am capable of self-control, even when it comes to you."

On the way to Jeff's apartment, I texted Donna asking her if she could take Bailey out for a walk. His place wasn't far from the restaurant, so we got to it a few minutes after he flagged down a taxi.

As I stepped inside his apartment I couldn't help but flash back to my first visit. The mental image of us in bed together made me want to get him out of his clothes now as badly as I had back then, but I wasn't about to tell him that.

Jeff hung up my coat and sat beside me on the couch. He rested his hand on my cheek, which was still flushed from the cold. "Have I ever told you how sexy you are?"

I bit my lower lip. "Nope. Never."

"Well you are." He scooted a few inches closer to me, leaned in and placed a soft, slow kiss on my lips. "I've missed you, you know."

Good Lord, I missed him too. That kiss he'd just given me wasn't going to be enough. Not by a mile. For the past few weeks I'd tried talking myself out of my attraction for him, out of how badly I wanted him, but he'd managed to wear me down and make me believe that he wanted the same things I did. I reached around the nape of his neck and pulled him close before pressing my lips on his. He responded by wrapping his arms around me and parting my lips with his tongue, deepening our kiss. We were supposed to be talking, I tried reminding myself, but that voice was drowned out by the heat spreading through my body. Jeff's hands moved quickly, reaching under my shirt. Mine moved faster, unbuttoning his. We made our way into his bedroom, dropping pieces of clothing along the way and doing our best not to trip over furniture. Jeff unzipped his pants and I reached for his erection.

"You see what you do to me?" he teased.

I took his hand and guided it between my legs so that he could feel that I was just as turned on as he was. My panties were still on, but I knew he could feel how wet I was for him through the fabric.

He moaned into my ear.

I stumbled backward and landed on the bed with Jeff on top of me. He practically tore my underwear off and then kneaded my breasts with his hands as he pressed his erection into me. I ran my hands up and down his back and opened my legs, wrapping them around his waist.

"I want you so bad," Jeff breathed.

"Then what are you waiting for?"

I didn't need to ask twice. Jeff slid inside me. The connection I felt as he moved back and forth, in and out, was dizzying. Sex with Jeff had always been amazing, but this time, knowing that what we were doing was more than just physical, that I meant something to him, made the link between us stronger than it ever had been. I felt sexy, desired, wanted.

He reached under me, cupping my ass with his hands and lifting me closer so he could drive his erection in even deeper. I gasped, then moaned with pleasure as he built up speed, leading me to climax. Every single nerve ending in my body tingled with electricity. A moment later Jeff climaxed. He pulled me close to him and I shuddered in his arms.

We lay quietly for a few minutes. With my head on his chest

I couldn't see his face, and I was desperately curious to see if I could read his expression, so I lifted my head to look at him. His eyes were closed and his lips were curled into a content smile.

I nudged him and his eyes flickered open. "I thought we were supposed to be talking," I said, jokingly.

"It's not my fault that you couldn't keep your hands off me."

"Hmph. You didn't put up much of a fight."

Jeff reached for me, smoothing my hair down with one of his hands. "Because I'm putty in your hands."

I laughed and lay my head back down on his chest. "Is that so?"

"You have no idea," he said, his voice barely louder than a whisper.

"That means I can ask you for a favor?"

"What kind of favor?"

"You have got to stop sending me flowers."

"Why?" Jeff asked, sounding insulted, which had not been my intention. "You don't like them?"

I lifted my head from Jeff's chest and lay on my side looking down at him. "No, that's not it at all. I love the flowers, they're so beautiful. But you've seen my apartment. It's not very big, I'm running out of room for all of them."

"Hmmm. That means I'll have to think of something else to send you. Maybe chocolate?"

I couldn't help but smile as I nestled back into the crook of his arm. How had I gotten this lucky? "I don't need any gifts, Jeff." He was present enough for me.

As the two of us lay there, I savored the silence, and the way the quiet made it possible for me to hear Jeff's heartbeat and the sound of his breathing.

But after a while I itched to know what was on his mind. "What are you thinking about?" I asked.

"That I should tell you that I got tested a few weeks ago. No STDs."

"I figured as much, since Dr. Lu told me all my results were normal."

"I just didn't want you to worry," he said.

"Did you know that's the first time I've ever done it without a condom?"

"I should've asked you first if it was okay."

"I would have stopped you if it wasn't," I reassured him.

"Susan . . ." Jeff paused; when I looked up at him, he continued. "If I call you my girlfriend, would that be cool?"

I almost felt like giggling. I hadn't felt this silly about a man in a long time. And it seemed like such a bizarre question considering the circumstances. Still, it was sweet the way he asked. "Only if I can call you my boyfriend."

Jeff gently scooted me off his chest and turned on his side, propping his head up with his arm. He stared down at me. "You'd better. Because this whole friends-with-benefits thing isn't for me. I'm not that kind of guy."

I shoved him playfully. "Are you making fun of me?"

"No." He leaned down and kissed me on the tip of my nose. "I would never do such a thing."

I looked away for a moment as a question I'd had on my mind for a while returned. I preferred joking around over serious discussions, but some things just needed to be asked. "What do you think your parents will say when you tell them about the baby?"

Jeff tucked a few stray strands of hair behind my ear. "My dad never says much about anything, so I'm not really worried about him. My mom, on the other hand—I'm not going to lie to you—she won't like it."

"She'll think I trapped you, won't she, that I'm after your money?"

"No, that's not it," Jeff said. "I mean, the thought might cross her mind, but I think most of all she'll be angry with me for not being more careful. In her mind there's a right way to go about having a child and a wrong way. My mom is still kind of old-fashioned that way. Marriage first, then baby."

"My mom's the same way," I said. "She'll flip when I tell her I'm pregnant."

"Wait a minute." Jeff had a surprised look on his face. "You still haven't told your parents?"

"There's only one parent to tell. My dad died when I was little," I explained. "But to answer your question, no, I haven't told my mom."

"Why not?"

"Hmmm, let me see," I said, sarcastically. "You try telling an Italian Catholic mother that her only child, who just got dumped by her fiancé, not only got knocked up, but she's not even sure by who."

"But you know now," Jeff said, stroking my cheek with his knuckles. "So you can leave that part of the story out. You're going to have to tell her eventually."

"I know. Believe me, I know. But every time I think I've worked up the courage to tell her, I chicken out."

"Maybe we can tell her together," Jeff suggested. "I've got to meet her at some point. If she sees how charming I am, perhaps she won't be as upset about the baby," he said with a grin.

"Excuse me, Mr. Modesty. You may be charming, but I don't think springing two surprises on my mother at the same time is a good idea. I need to tell her about the baby first. Once she gets over the shock, she'll want to meet you, and probably make me invite you over for one of her famous Italian dinners."

"Will she hate me?"

"How can she? You're far too charming," I said, smiling.

Jeff laughed. And the next thing I knew laughter led to kissing, and kissing led to touching, and then we were both too turned on to do anything else except make love again.

"Promise me something," Jeff said afterward.

"Okay. What is it?"

"That you'll be here in the morning when I wake up."

I smiled, thinking back to our first night together and realizing how wrong I'd been to leave, assuming things about him I shouldn't have. I was grateful that we were beyond that now. "Don't worry," I said. "I'll be here."

Chapter 20
Breaking the News

Jesse called the next day while Jeff and I were in the kitchen eating a breakfast of scrambled eggs and toast he'd cooked for us. My phone was closest to Jeff so he picked it up when he saw Jesse's name displayed across the screen.

"Good morning, Jesse," he said casually. I could hear her practically squealing through the phone's speaker. I tried to pry my phone out of Jeff's hands, but he held on to it firmly.

"At least put it on speaker phone," I grumbled.

"Oh you'd like that, wouldn't you?" he whispered before pressing the phone back to his ear. "Where was I?" he said. "Oh, yeah. I was about to tell you, my *sister-in-law*, some news."

"I should be the one to tell her." I tried to grab the phone from him again.

He just grinned and ducked out of reach.

"So Susan and I are officially dating."

Another loud squeal came from the phone.

"Speakerphone," I insisted.

This time Jeff pulled the phone away from his ear and laid it down on the countertop before pressing the speaker button.

"And we're going to have a baby," he said "But you probably knew that already."

"Wait, what? I feel like I'm missing something here," Jesse said.

I hadn't told Jesse about getting the DNA test done. I'd been too nervous about what the result would be to talk about it. Jeff filled her in on the details of my last OB appointment and the blood test that I'd had. It was embarrassing to hear the words spoken aloud by Jeff, even though I knew there was no reason to be ashamed. When Jeff and I had sex the first time, he knew it had only been days since my breakup with Greg.

"Oh my God, I'm so freaking excited for you guys," Jesse said, almost breathless. "I can't believe that I'm officially going to be an aunt in a few months. Does this mean I can finally tell Justin?"

I looked at Jeff. "You haven't said anything to your brother?"

"I wanted to wait until you said it was okay."

For some reason that really touched me—that Jeff was able to keep such a huge piece of news to himself until I gave him the okay to share it. I wrapped my arms around him and planted a kiss on his lips. "You're awesome."

"Hello, are you guys still there?" Jesse asked.

I pulled away from Jeff, laughing. "Yeah, we're here," I said. "Go ahead and tell Justin if you want to."

"You know what? It's your news. You guys should be the one to tell him. Are you at Jeff's place now, or yours?"

"Jeff's," I said.

"Good. We'll be there in ten minutes."

Without giving me a chance to protest, Jesse hung up. The

only clothes I had with me were the ones I'd been wearing the day before. I might not have minded facing Jesse while wearing a pair of Jeff's boxers and one of his shirts, but with Justin coming over I preferred showering and putting on my own clothes.

A few minutes after I finished dressing Jesse and Justin arrived. The first thing Jesse did was rush over to me with her arms open.

"Can somebody tell me what the heck is going on already?" Justin said.

We exchanged glances at each other, waiting to see who was going to speak first.

"He's your brother," Jesse said to Jeff, "you should be the one to tell him."

"Okay." Jeff walked over to me and snaked his arm around my waist. "What's going on is that Sue and I are dating. We're officially boyfriend and girlfriend." A smile spread across his face.

"So you finally agreed to go out with my loser brother?" Justin quipped.

"There's more," Jeff said, gearing up to drop his bombshell. He glanced down at me before continuing, "We're also having a baby."

We all just stared at Justin, waiting to see what his reaction would be. His eyes flicked back and forth among the three of us as if he were trying to figure out if we were pranking him. "You're kidding me, right?"

"Nope, Uncle. I'm totally not," Jeff said.

Justin's expression morphed from shock to joy. "Holy crap, I can't believe this." He crossed the room and gave his brother a hug first, then me. "You do know Mom's going to kill you, right?" He looked at me over Jeff's shoulder. "No offense, Susan."

The idea of Mrs. Lambert being displeased did not sit well with me.

"She will not kill him," Jesse protested. "Allison might be a bit cold at first, but once you get to know her, she's not that bad."

"I just don't think my mom is ready to have anyone call her Grandma yet."

"Justin, that's ridiculous," Jesse said. "It's not like you guys are teenagers."

"I'm not worried about what Mom's going to think," Jeff said. "She's going to do what she always does—freak out—then realize that she's totally overreacting and come to her senses. Besides, right about now, I'm too damn happy to worry about Mom." He turned to look at me. "You're happy too, babe, right?"

Babe? That was a new one. And kind of cute.

"Yeah," I said, realizing that it really was true. "I am."

"So when's your due date?" Justin asked.

"July fifteenth."

I could see the wheels in Justin's mind turning as he calculated the timing of things. "Exactly how far along are you?" he finally asked.

"About thirteen weeks."

Jeff smiled and pulled me closer. "Let's just say we found a good way to celebrate your wedding."

Justin stared at Jesse. "You knew about this the whole time, didn't you?"

"Sort of," she replied sheepishly.

"In Jesse's defense," I said, "I made her promise not to say anything to anyone."

"So I was basically busting my ass trying to figure out how to hook the two of you up when you guys were already together?"

Jesse chuckled. "Believe me, Justin, you do not even want the two of them to answer that question," she said.

The four of us talked for a while longer. Jesse wanted to plan some shopping days for maternity clothes and baby things, and also to set a date for my baby shower, but I wasn't ready to think that far ahead. I still had to figure out how to tell my mother and then my boss. Something I really couldn't put off for much longer.

After Jesse and Justin left, I turned to Jeff. "I should get going too."

He frowned. "Do you really have to?"

"It's not that I don't want to stay," I replied. "But I've got Bailey and the dogs that need walking, and I don't want to wear the same clothes three days in a row."

"I thought you were planning on giving up dog-walking now that you have a full-time job."

"I need to give my clients time to find someone else first."

"That's awfully nice of you," he said, wrapping his arms around me. "Say I'll get to see you again soon."

"Of course you will." I rested my head on his chest for a moment before looking up at him. That was one of my favorite things about Jeff, how tall he was.

"Let me get you a cab ride home."

"That's not necessary. I'm perfectly capable of taking the train."

"Yeah, but you're pregnant."

"And I'll be pregnant for the next six months. There's no way I can afford taxi rides everywhere for that long."

"Well, how about just this once, then."

I relented, appreciating that I wouldn't have to deal with the weekend train service.

Jeff called a few hours after I got back home. "I've got a great idea," he said. "How about Friday night we both break the news to our parents about the baby. And then Saturday night gets to be ours. We can share our war stories."

I had to laugh. War story was not an exaggeration. "My mom is so going to kill me."

"Then on second thought, don't tell her. We can both run away and start a new life on some tropical island. No one has to know."

"And ruin all of Jesse's baby shower plans? There's no way I could do that."

He chuckled. "Yeah, you're right. Knowing her and Justin, they'd find a way to track us down."

"I've been psyching myself up all afternoon to call my mom," I said. "I can totally do this."

Telling my mother over the phone was a no-no, though. So after Jeff and I finished talking, I called her and invited her to come over on Friday after I got off work.

~

Unlike my mother, I didn't really like cooking and wasn't very good at it, so on my way home from work that Friday I picked up takeout Chinese. I'd just begun to set the small table in my kitchen—my mother was not the type of person who ate out of takeout containers with plastic cutlery—when she tapped at the door.

Mom removed her coat while I transferred the contents of four white boxes onto plates— rice, lo mein, orange chicken, and beef and broccoli. My mom kept looking at me out of the corner of her eye. "You need to tell me something, don't you?" she finally said.

"How did you know?"

"I'm your mother, that's how."

I sat down, shook a pair of wooden chopsticks free from the paper sleeve they came in, and snapped them apart. Somehow keeping my hands busy helped to calm my frayed nerves.

"Well, out with it already. You're making your poor mother nervous."

One big bite of noodles and a huge gulp of water was all I needed to propel myself forward. I finished chewing then set my chopsticks down in front of me. "I'm pregnant."

My mom stared at me for a moment, first looking surprised, then annoyed. "Susan Calabro. If you think trying to give your poor mother a heart attack is funny, I can assure you it is not."

"I'm not trying to be funny, or give you a heart attack. I just thought you might want to know that in another six months you're going to have a grandchild."

The look on my mother's face was indecipherable. Shock, anger, disappointment? One thing was certain, joy didn't come into it. "How is this even possible?"

I gave her a quizzical look. "Do I really need to explain? I know it may have been awhile for you and all, but not much has changed when it comes to the way babies are made."

"That's not what I meant and you know it," my mother said, growing impatient. "I'm just wondering why you never bothered to tell me you and Greg had gotten back together."

"Because we didn't," I said, casually, hoping that if I sounded nonchalant, somehow that attitude would transfer over to my mother. "The baby isn't Greg's."

The color drained from my mom's face. She got up from the table. "Susan, this is not the woman I raised you to be. Please tell me you are joking."

I was half-tempted to give my mother my opinion on her old-fashioned ideas of what exactly a woman was supposed to act like. This was the twenty-first century, not the eighteen hundreds. But I didn't want to get into an argument, and I could sense that's where we were headed if I didn't try to explain my side of things.

"My relationship with Greg was really over long before he moved out. I'd been feeling lonely for months. So when Jeff came along, it was like we had this almost instant connection. I felt rejected by the way Greg left me, and Jeff made me feel special . . . he just made things better. He was what I needed."

"So you just jumped into bed with this . . ." My mom waved one of her hands in the air. "Jeff?"

There was no use arguing that point since it was actually a pretty accurate description. Maybe the way Jeff and I had gotten together wasn't well thought out, but it had happened, and by some strange luck, things were working between us. "Listen, I know this is a shock, but I'm happy. I really like Jeff, and even though I was scared at first when I found out I was pregnant, now I'm excited."

My mother shook her head. "I don't even know what to say."

"Say you're happy. You've been bugging me about wanting to be a grandmother for years. Now your wish is finally coming true."

"I suppose," my mom said, as if genuinely pondering my words. "This is definitely not the way I pictured things happening. But what's done is done and you're right, I do want to be a grandma. I just hope this Jeff character doesn't wind up disappointing you the way Greg did."

"There is one other thing I should tell you," I said. "You need to know that just because I'm pregnant it doesn't mean I'm getting married."

My mother frowned. "Somehow I figured you were going to say that."

I waited for her to lift her eyes from her plate. "I think you'll really like Jeff."

"Where exactly did the two of you meet?"

"You remember my friend, Jesse, right?" Mom nodded, and I continued, "He's her brother-in-law."

"So you got yourself a stuffy city boy?"

My mom had lived in Brooklyn her entire life. She could hop on the train and be in Manhattan in under an hour, yet I could probably count on one hand how many times she'd headed into the city over the past few years. She thumbed her nose at anyone she considered phony, and I knew the Lamberts would fall squarely into that category. But Jeff was charming, and I was certain he'd win her over.

"He's not stuffy, he's funny." Smiling, I got up to give my mom a kiss on her cheek. "You'll see."

Chapter 21
Meeting Mothers

The next evening, as planned, Jeff and I shared our stories about the way our parents had reacted to our baby news. It sounded like my mother had taken the news better than Jeff's had.

"Like I told you would happen, my dad didn't have much to say," he said. "My mom, on the other hand, well, she wasn't exactly what I'd call happy."

"What did she say?" I asked, trying to hide how disappointed his news made me feel.

Jeff chuckled. "Quite a bit. It's a good thing I've got all night to tell you about it," he said. "Predictably, she started with the whole 'you're too young' bit; from there she went on and on about not being ready to be a grandmother, but that even if she was Justin and Jesse were supposed to have a baby first, since Justin is older and married. Then she finished off with a lecture about how much smarter my brother was for not rushing into being a parent."

"Ouch. Sounds like you got an earful."

Jeff shrugged. "I was expecting it. It's not a big deal. My mother is very opinionated, but eventually she'll come around."

"My mom was pretty upset about the whole not being married thing, too," I said. "And she wasn't happy about you being a snooty rich kid either."

"Wait a minute." Jeff looked up from his plate. "You told your mother I was a snooty rich kid?"

"No, of course I didn't. That's just what she assumed when I explained how the two of us had met."

"That's just great. I haven't even met your mother yet, and she already hates me."

"She does not," I protested. "Besides, if anyone here has to worry about someone's mother hating them, it's me."

Jeff shook his head. "At least you've already met my mom. And anyway, it's not you she's mad at, it's me."

"She remembers me?" I wasn't sure why that surprised me as much as it did.

"You were the maid of honor at her son's wedding; of course she remembers you."

"Did she say anything about me?" I asked, hoping I wouldn't regret my curiosity.

"Her exact words?"

I nodded.

"She thinks you're pretty, and down to earth"

"She does?"

Jeff nodded. I sat back in my chair. At least Mrs. Lambert had good things to say about me. After everything I'd heard from Jesse about her mother-in-law, I expected her to accuse me of getting pregnant on purpose just to extort money from her son. Perhaps she wasn't quite as paranoid when it came to Jeff as she had been with Justin.

"So what now?" I asked.

"I should meet your mother."

"I hope you like Italian food."

Jeff smiled. "Who doesn't?"

"Good, because meeting my mom means a huge home-cooked dinner where you'll be expected to not only empty your entire plate but ooh and ahh over how amazing everything tastes."

"Is that all?" Jeff said. "I can totally do that."

"Perfect." I smiled. "Because I told my mom we'd be over tomorrow after church."

"I can't wait." Instead of being nervous, Jeff seemed excited at the prospect. I envied his self-confidence.

The next day, as we rode the train to my mom's house, I wished for a little bit of that self-confidence for myself. I couldn't help but worry about what my mother would think of Jeff. What was she going to say when she realized how much younger he was than me? Our age difference wasn't really apparent to most people because I looked a lot younger than I was, but there would be no fooling my mom, who, of course, knew exactly how old I was.

I tried to ignore my racing heart as I rang her doorbell. She opened the door a few seconds later with Frank standing right behind her, and hurriedly ushered us inside so that we wouldn't let all the heat out.

After removing our coats and shoes, I made the introductions.

Jeff gave Frank a firm handshake and my mother a kiss on the cheek. Clearly he'd been brushing up on Italian customs. "Nice to meet you, Mrs. Calabro," he told her.

"It's nice to meet you as well." My mom was being more polite than I had anticipated she'd be.

"It smells so good in here," Jeff said as she led us into the living room where we all took seats.

"Anna is a great cook," Frank said, patting his belly. "I must have gained at least ten pounds since the two of us met."

My mom loved getting compliments on her cooking. She smiled at Frank before turning her attention to Jeff. "So, Jeff, Susan tells me you're some sort of banker?"

"My official title is wealth manager. I help people figure out how invest their money."

"Must be a nice problem, having so much money that you need to hire someone to help you decide what to do with it all."

Jeff shrugged, unperturbed by the sarcasm in my mother's voice. "It's definitely a nice problem for me, since that's how I pay my bills."

Jeff's attempt at humor elicited a chuckle from Frank, which he quickly stifled when he noticed my mom's serious expression. I sensed her gearing up for another question. "Mom," I said, "we just got here. Can you save the interrogation for later?"

"Asking a few questions is hardly an interrogation."

"Nope," Frank said. "Not the same thing at all."

"That's not helping," I said.

"Well, if anyone should know, it's Frank. He used to interrogate people all the time when he was a police officer," my mom said, almost beaming with pride.

The two of them made such an adorable couple, and I loved that my mom had found someone after so many years of being alone, but I didn't appreciate the two of them teaming up against me.

"Questions don't bother me," Jeff said.

"Good, because I have plenty of them. But they'll have to wait. I don't want to burn lunch." My mom stood up. "Susan, can you give me a hand in the kitchen?"

Subtlety was not my mother's strong suit. It was pretty obvious she was trying to get me alone to discuss something in private. I followed her into the kitchen with a glance over my shoulder at Jeff, who had already been drawn into Frank's favorite topic of discussion, his career with the NYPD.

"I already know what you're going to say, so don't bother," I said.

My mother frowned. "You do not."

"You're going to tell me you don't like Jeff," I said. "You never like anyone I date."

"That's not true," my mother insisted. "I liked Greg."

"Not at first, you didn't."

"How old is Jeff?"

I contemplated stretching the truth, adding a few numbers to Jeff's age, but if my mother caught me in a lie I'd never hear the end of it. I hadn't intended on falling for someone eight years younger, but it had happened, and feelings weren't just something you could undo. "He's twenty-four," I replied. "But before you start lecturing me about him being too young, you can just save it. Whatever you're about to tell me, I've already told myself a hundred times."

My mother shrugged. "There's no point. Whether I like it or not, he's the father of that baby you're carrying. That's not something that can be undone."

"No, it can't. So can we stop talking about it?" I could read all of my mother's unspoken thoughts, and whether I wanted them to or not, they were setting off all kinds of panicky fears in me about Jeff that I'd sworn I'd already gotten over.

"Fine. Why don't you help me get some salad ready?"

I knew where everything was, so I grabbed a bowl and the ingredients I needed from the refrigerator, and started chopping. I was almost done when my mom looked over her shoulder at me. "Jeff is a handsome young man."

I smiled. "He's more than that, Mom. He's really funny, and he makes me feel special. I was so sure he'd freak out about me getting pregnant, but he didn't. He's actually excited about being a dad."

My mom walked over to me and put her arms around me. She kissed me on my forehead. "The more you talk about being pregnant, the more real this whole thing is starting to get. I can't wait for your baby to get here."

"Stop, Mom," I teased. "If we both go back out there crying the guys will think we're crazy."

"You're right." My mother dabbed her eyes with the back of her hand. She handed me the bowl of salad I'd just finished making. "Why don't you take this out to the dining room table?"

A few minutes later she called Jeff and Frank to the table, and the four of us sat down. Mom said grace before we started to eat.

"This is seriously the best meal I've ever had," Jeff said after a few bites.

"I told you she was a good cook." Frank winked at my mom.

"Italian food is pretty simple," she said. "I'm sure your mother cooked a lot of pasta when you were a kid."

"No." Jeff shook his head. "My mother doesn't cook."

Mom frowned. "Then how did you eat?"

"Let's just put it this way. I pretty much grew up on takeout."

Jeff's statement was practically sacrilegious to my mother, who believed that a home-cooked meal was the answer to pretty much all of life's problems, but thankfully she kept that to herself. My mother's behavior with Jeff was so unexpected. Aside from the few awkward moments right after Jeff and I arrived, lunch had gone well—no third degree, no preaching. By the time dessert was brought out I'd let myself relax, certain that the hardest part was over.

But then my mother turned to look at Jeff and asked him, "So have the two of you talked about what your living arrangements will be after the baby comes?"

I almost choked on my last bite of cake.

"We haven't really made any decisions yet," Jeff said.

Mom's eyes widened. "The baby will be here before you know it. You two need to start making plans for him or her now. A baby changes your life in ways you can't even begin to imagine."

"Mom, come on. Jeff and I are both adults. We'll sort everything out."

Frank cleared his throat and lifted his wine glass. "A toast," he said, clearly trying to steer my mom off the course she'd gotten onto. "To Jeff and Susan and the baby they are about to have." He glanced at my mother who, despite the forced smile on her face, also lifted her glass.

After my mom had brought up the uncomfortable subject of living arrangements, I couldn't wait to get back home. I made an excuse about Bailey needing a walk and piles of laundry that needed to be folded. My mom must have sensed that I was annoyed with her, so she didn't try and convince me to stay longer.

It was another super cold afternoon, so when Jeff and I got back to my apartment he generously offered to walk Bailey for me. When they got back, he sat beside me on the couch while Bailey plopped himself down at my feet, warming my cold toes with his body.

"Next time you spend the weekend at my place, you should bring Bailey," Jeff said as he wrapped an arm around me.

"Are you serious?"

"I told you, I always wanted a dog."

I gave Jeff a kiss. "You're so sweet."

He grinned. "I'm glad you think so."

I rested my head on his chest and for a few minutes we just sat there, silently, until Jeff said, "What are you thinking about?"

"That I really wish I had a fireplace."

"Are you cold?" Jeff asked, pulling me closer to him. "Because if you are, I can think of a few ways to keep you warm."

"No. I'm not cold. I've just always loved the idea of sitting in front of a fire in the winter with a cup of hot chocolate and a good book."

"That does sound nice." With his free hand, Jeff laced his fingers through mine.

"What about you?" I asked. "What are you thinking about?"

"About what your mother said."

"She said a lot of things," I mumbled.

"Yeah, but you know what I'm talking about," he said. "She's right. We need to start thinking about what's going to happen after the baby comes. You and me, and of course Bailey, should be living together; that's the only thing that makes sense."

I avoided his gaze. "If I wasn't pregnant, would we even be having this conversation?"

"But you are pregnant, so what does it matter?"

"It matters to me. Living with someone is a big deal, and not something we should just rush into because of the baby. Plenty of people co-parent without living together."

"Yes, but those people aren't usually couples," Jeff pointed out.

He was right, but our baby wasn't due until the summer. Which meant we had plenty of time to make such a huge decision. "I just don't want to rush into anything."

"It's a bit too late for that, wouldn't you say?"

"Neither of us planned on having a baby. It wasn't a decision we actively made. Moving in together is," I said.

Jeff rested his hand on my cheek. "I'm not going to pressure you. I just want you to know that I'm not asking because of the baby. I really like you, and I like spending time with you. Moving in together just makes sense."

Like, not love. There was a huge difference. I had no right to expect more than what Jeff had given me up to now. Love took time, and until we both felt it, I just couldn't say yes to living with him. Not after the disastrous way things had ended between me and Greg.

I gave Jeff a forced smile before saying, "I like spending time with you, too."

He reached his hand around the nape of my neck and pulled me into a kiss. I wrapped my arms around him and kissed him back, harder, deeper. I expected him to take me into the bedroom, but instead he pulled back.

"What's wrong?" I asked.

"There's something I've been meaning to give you," he said, reaching into his pocket.

He handed me a small velvet box. I wasn't expecting a present. Especially not jewelry. "You didn't have to," I said

"Just open it."

Hesitantly, I opened the lid. Inside lay a delicate platinum chain with three disc-shaped pendants. One was engraved with the letter S, the other with the letter J. As I lifted it from the box, Jeff said, "My initial and yours. The third one's blank. We can get it engraved with our baby's initial after he comes."

I started to tear up. It was one of the most thoughtful presents I'd ever received.

"Do you like it?" Jeff asked.

I glanced at him. "I love it. It's the nicest present anyone's ever given me."

Jeff took the necklace from my hands and put it around my neck. I fingered the small pendants while he fixed the clasp.

"What makes you think our baby is going to be a boy?" I asked when he was done.

Jeff looked pensive. "I don't really know why I said that, since I'm actually hoping for a cute, curly-haired girl who looks just like you."

I smiled. "Jeff, I love the necklace. It's perfect."

~

The following weekend, it was my turn for a family get-together with Jeff's parents. I'd hoped Jesse and Justin would be there for moral support, but they'd made plans to spend the weekend away from the city. James wasn't there either, since the winter semester had already started and he was back in Connecticut where he went to college.

Mrs. Lambert asked us over for brunch. I'd been invited to two separate parties at the Lamberts' apartment, but those had been outside, on their rooftop deck. This time brunch was served inside their home. Jesse's description of the place hadn't done it any justice. I tried not to gawk, and Mrs. Lambert was polite enough not to comment on how clearly in awe I was of the lavishness of my surroundings. Everything they owned, from their furniture to the area rug I stood on, seemed high-end.

I'd expected Jeff's mother to ask the same question my mother had about what Jeff and I planned to do after the baby came. She didn't. If anything she seemed rather detached, as if brunch was just a formality she had to get through. I remembered Jesse warning me that it took Mrs. Lambert time to warm up to people. I didn't let her aloofness really get to me, though. Of course I wanted her to like me, but I had plenty of my own family to deal with, so I appreciated the way Mrs. Lambert refrained from offering her opinions. Still, by the time Jeff and I left, I was mentally exhausted.

At least we had gotten over one more hurdle. Not that long ago things had seemed so bleak, but now I had a full-time job I loved, Jeff and I were together, happy, and excited about our baby that would be here in another few months. Bit by bit it felt like things were shifting into place; that the storm I'd been in the middle of for the past few months was finally beginning to clear.

Chapter 22
Names . . . And Other Things

My life settled into a routine. I'd finally worked up the courage to tell my boss about the baby. Surprisingly, Linda was very understanding, only saying that she hoped I'd return to work after the baby was born. I finally gave up dog walking so Bailey and I were able to spend entire weekends with Jeff at his apartment.

I had another OB appointment and finally found time to go shopping for maternity clothing. Besides getting too big for all my old clothes, my body started changing in other ways. Morning sickness was really and truly over, and I was no longer tired all the time. If anything, I had more energy than before. And I began to feel my baby kicking. But as exciting as that was, what I really looked forward to was my next ultrasound. On my last appointment Dr. Lu had explained that the fetus would be a lot bigger, and we'd even get to discover the baby's gender if we wanted to know.

I hadn't given much thought to whether I'd prefer a boy or a girl. People were constantly guessing what I'd have, and I found myself wanting to ask them why it mattered. Which is why by the time my next appointment with Dr. Lu came around I decided to tell her that I wanted to be surprised and find out what I was having after I gave birth, not before. I peered over Dr. Lu's shoulder to ask Jeff if he was okay with that. He mulled over the question for a bit before replying. "No," he said. "I don't mind, because truthfully, I don't care. All I want is a healthy baby."

And that's what Dr. Lu said we were going to have after finishing up my ultrasound. At twenty weeks I was halfway through my pregnancy. The baby was developing normally, had a strong heart, and all the right parts in all the right places. Seeing him or her on the ultrasound monitor, moving around, almost brought tears to my eyes. Jeff seemed equally moved as we watched the way our baby kept its fists clenched and pressed against his or her cheeks.

"Have you guys decided on any names yet?" Dr. Lu asked.

"I haven't." Jeff reached for my hand. "Have you thought of anything?"

I shook my head. With all the craziness that had been going on during the first few months of my pregnancy, names had been the last thing on my mind. "Not really."

"You should be the one to decide," Jeff said. "Except no J names. We've already got too many of those in my family."

"Let me leave the two of you alone to finish this discussion," Dr. Lu said, getting up from her stool. "I'll see you two in another four weeks, okay?"

After setting up my next appointment, Jeff and I went to get lunch. While we waited for our food, Jeff reached across the table for my hand. I looked up at him, waiting to hear what was on his mind.

"The baby will be here in a few months, Sue. We really have to start thinking about names . . . among other things."

"What other things?"

"I think you should reconsider moving in with me," he said. "Your apartment is too small, and you're not going to feel like lugging a stroller up and down those steps every day."

"You're right. I'm not going to like it," I conceded. "But I'm not moving in with you just to get out of climbing a couple of flights of steps. That isn't a reason to live with someone." I got that Jeff was trying to be practical, but I didn't want practical. I wanted passion, fire. I wanted Jeff to tell me the reason we should live together was because he hated not waking up next to me each morning, not because it made sense.

"Why is it so hard to convince you that moving in together is the right thing to do?"

"I think we should wait until the baby is here and see how we feel then."

Jeff shook his head. "What's it going to take to get it through your head that I'm committed to you, to this baby, to us?"

"Why are you mad?" I asked, sensing his frustration. "Most guys would be thrilled not to be pushed into something before they were ready."

"Just because this pregnancy wasn't planned, doesn't mean I'm not ready."

"And I don't see the harm in waiting a little bit longer." Things were going so well between us that I didn't want to rock the boat. I liked the way things were. "Moving in together is a big commitment. I don't want to rush things."

For a moment I thought he'd argue with me, but instead he

leaned back in his chair. "Fine. I won't bring it up again." His expression softened. "But can we at least think of some names?"

I rested my hands on my belly. Our baby was kicking around in there. "I'm not sure about boy names, but if it's a girl, I've always like the name Elena."

"Elena?" Jeff thought about it for a moment. "I like it. It's different, without being weird. But what if it's not a girl?"

"I don't know. What do you think?"

"What about Spencer?"

"Spencer?" I shook my head. "I don't think so."

We tossed a few more names around, but didn't come up with anything I really liked. Boy names were hard, and since Jeff and I had a few more months to think of something, we eventually gave up trying.

Over the next few weeks my mom, Jesse, and Mrs. Lambert started slowly loading me up with gifts. I stacked them in a corner of my living room, and every night when I came home from work something about seeing them there sent both a thrill and a heart-hammering fear running through me. I was both excited and petrified at the same time about the baby. My mom convinced me to enroll in prenatal classes so I'd have some idea of what to expect. Jesse and I went to Target and Babies R Us so I could get baby registries started up. I started looking through the disability and family leave papers my boss had given me. Technically, I hadn't worked at Promises long enough to earn maternity leave, but my boss told me she'd give it to me anyway.

From my mom to the cashier at the bagel shop, it seemed like everywhere I went I got all kinds of advice from well-meaning people. They told me to enjoy my pregnancy, to make sure I got as much sleep as I could because after the baby was born my life would never be the same. So I did my best to savor each day. I appreciated every little baby kick, every weekend with Jeff, the calls from Jesse and my mom checking in on me, even my job and those cute little four-year-old faces I saw every day.

And then one afternoon, right before Jeff was about to leave town on another business trip, the happiness I'd foolishly let myself get used to came to a screeching halt.

Chapter 23
Nina

All I wanted to do was call Jeff to wish him a safe trip. He was going to be gone for a little over a week. This time his work was sending him all the way to Singapore. He hadn't even left yet and I already missed him. I wanted to tell him that before he got on a plane that would take him halfway around the world.

During my lunch break I dialed his number, but it wasn't his voice that came on the other end of the phone, it was a woman's. Puzzled, I checked to make sure I'd dialed correctly, but it was definitely Jeff's name displayed across my phone's screen.

"Who is this?" I asked.

"Nina," the woman replied casually. "And you would be?"

Nina? Jeff's ex? There was no freaking way. What was she doing answering his phone? "Where's Jeff?" I said, trying to keep my voice from trembling.

"Um . . . he's kind of busy right now. Do you want me to give him a message?"

It wasn't only what she said, but the way she said it, that made me feel like all the blood had drained from my head. I couldn't think straight, but somehow I managed to say, "Can you tell him Susan called?"

"Sure, yeah. I can do that," Nina said in a sing-song voice before hanging up on me. It almost felt like she sensed my displeasure and was reveling in it.

I tried to stifle the panic that spread through me. What was Nina doing answering Jeff's phone? He was my Jeff, not hers. It didn't mean anything. At least that's what I tried telling myself. I sat down with my phone in my hand, convinced that Jeff would call me back any minute. When he did, I'd demand to know what he was doing with Nina and he'd give me some explanation that made sense, even though I couldn't think of a single one.

As the minutes ticked by I contemplated catching a cab and going to Jeff's apartment to demand answers. But I was at work, and my lunch break would be over in a few minutes. I couldn't just leave; I had a room full of four-year-olds who needed me to keep an eye on them at recess and read them their favorite *Pete the Cat* book after.

After what felt like the slowest four hours ever, I left work and headed to the train station. Jeff's flight took off in less than an hour, which meant he was probably in the middle of a long security line at LaGuardia airport. Why hadn't he left me a message or at least a text like he always did before he went on a business trip? Once he got on the plane, who knew when I'd hear from him? The flight to Singapore would be a long one. *If* he was even going on a business trip. What if he'd only told me that as a cover, a way to spend the week with Nina without me suspecting anything?

I made myself sick with theories about why Jeff's ex had answered his phone. Even after I got home I couldn't stop thinking about it, no matter how hard I'd tried to distract myself.

Tired of torturing myself, I decided to take Bailey on a long walk to clear my head. It was freezing outside, but somehow my anger at Jeff fueled me forward. I kept walking until finally the cold and sheer exhaustion got the better of me.

When I got back to my apartment I picked up right where I'd left off, brooding over Jeff and Nina and whatever the heck was going on between them. Try as I might I simply couldn't come up with a reasonable explanation for why Nina had answered Jeff's phone or why he hadn't bothered to call me before getting on the plane.

I truly believed I'd been making Jeff happy, but the more I thought about it, the more I realized that something between us had changed, and it all began after my last OB appointment, the one where I'd had my ultrasound, the day I'd told Jeff I wasn't ready to move in with him.

The changes were subtle enough that like an idiot, I hadn't noticed them, even though after everything that had happened with Greg, I totally should have. Jeff was still a passionate lover, generous not only in bed, but with gifts and affection. But he'd become more of a casual observer when it came to decisions about our relationship and the baby. When I asked what he thought about a design for the baby's room, he just shrugged his shoulders and told me that whatever I liked was fine. And he always let me be the one to decide where to eat or whether or not one of us would spend the night at the other's apartment. Was it because he'd begun to lose interest in me? Could something as simple as me saying no to moving in together be enough to make him reconsider his feelings for me? I didn't want to believe our relationship could be that fragile.

I wondered if Nina had even told Jeff that I'd called. And if she had, did he care that I was sitting at home trying to figure out what to do with the shreds of my heart? I'd been angry when Greg moved out, pissed when I found out he'd left me for someone else. But this was different, because I didn't have the same feelings for Greg that I had for Jeff. Even though I hadn't told Jeff, I was desperately and maddeningly in love with him. Everything, from the way his blue eyes lit up a room to the way he made me laugh, had captured my heart, but I'd been so afraid of losing him, of driving him away, that I hadn't told him.

My thoughts had turned into such an ugly stew of anger and heartache that I couldn't take it anymore. I broke down and called Jesse. She didn't answer, and after I hung up the phone I was relieved she hadn't. Drawing her into this was the last thing our friendship needed. But since I was at a breaking point and desperate to talk to someone, I called my mom.

"What's the matter?" she asked, hearing the despair in my voice.

"I'm pretty sure Jeff's decided to get back together with his ex," I said, failing in my effort not to cry. As I blurted out the whole story, tears starting falling fast and furious.

"What? How could he do that at a time like this? You're about to have his baby, for God's sake." I could hear the anger in my mother's voice. She could be super protective of me sometimes, like a mama bear defending her cub. Right now, that was exactly what I needed.

"This baby wasn't exactly planned, Mom, you know that. Maybe he realized it was all too much for him."

"Have you had a chance to hear his side of things?"

"No, Mom. I told you the last time I talked to him was this morning before I left for work."

"I'm not as convinced as you are that Jeff is reconciling with that Nina girl. Perhaps you should give him a chance to explain what happened."

"He had his chance to explain before he got on the plane, but he didn't return my call. That's enough explanation for me."

My mother sighed. "I was afraid something like this would happen. He's so young."

"You and Dad were young when you had me. Why should that make a difference?"

"Well, unfortunately, things have changed a lot since those days," she said. "People don't seem to care as much about honoring their commitments."

I felt fairly certain that Jeff actually would honor his commitment to me and the baby. When he got back from Singapore, he'd still want to come with me to my doctor appointments, and be there when our baby was born, but that had never been what I'd wanted from him. My worst fears were coming true, that Jeff would do what he believed was the right thing by me, but that's where it would end. Why had I let him in, when I knew this was going to happen? I couldn't explain to my mother how utterly devastated I felt. She was far too pragmatic to understand. "Mom, what am I going to do?"

"You're going to raise that baby of yours on your own, that's what. You'll have me to help you. You have your job, and health insurance; everything will be fine."

Except it wouldn't be. Because the only thing I could think about was the deep, dark hole my life would be without Jeff in it. I imagined myself handing our child over to him every other weekend, I pictured Nina being the one to see my baby take his or her first step or hear my baby's first word instead of getting to experience those things for myself with Jeff beside me. All those dreams I'd had of the two of us together when our baby came into this world, of being a family, the three of us, lay shattered at my feet. I would go on. I had to, but without Jeff I really didn't feel like it.

Before I had a chance to respond to my mom's pep talk there was a knock at my door. "Mom, someone's here. I've got to go."

"Okay, honey. Call me back if you need to talk some more."

I hung up, wiped the tears from my eyes and got up to answer the door. Donna stepped inside my apartment with a gift bag in her hands. "Since you never come by the bar anymore, I decided to bring this to you."

I took the bag from her hands. "Thank you, you didn't have to," I said, closing the door and ushering her inside. "Have a seat. Do you want something to drink?"

"No," she said, "I'm good."

I set the present down in the corner of my living room with the rest of the baby's gifts.

"Is everything okay?" Donna asked. "You look like you've been crying."

"I'm fine. It's just hard to get enough sleep with this giant belly of mine," I said. "That's probably why my eyes are so puffy."

Donna seemed to accept my explanation. She gestured toward the present she'd brought. "I want you to open it."

I picked the bag she'd given me back up and plucked out

sheet after sheet of tissue paper, before lifting the present out. It was a ten-by-twelve photo frame with four open squares. One for baby's ultrasound, another for footprints. On the bottom were supposed to go baby's first picture, and a photo of Mom and Dad. I started crying.

Donna got up to give me a hug. "Pregnancy hormones?"

I nodded. Donna was a friend, but we weren't close the way I was with Jesse. I couldn't bring myself to tell her why the frame had made me cry. It took me a moment, but I managed to pull myself together. "It's really beautiful," I said. "Thank you."

"I found it at this tiny baby store in the city and just had to get it for you. I wanted to buy you something unique."

"Thank you," I said, giving her a weak smile. "I've never seen anything like it."

"Well, I should probably head back downstairs. My shift starts soon."

I walked her to the door. She turned around just as she was about to head down the stairs. "One more thing. First drink after you have that baby is on me."

I smiled. "Thanks, Donna. I plan on taking you up on that."

Chapter 24
Deja Vu

Jeff finally called almost twenty-four hours after his flight had taken off. But I was so angry and hurt I just couldn't bring myself to pick up the phone. A long distance call from Singapore hardly seemed like the ideal way to hash things out with the father of my baby, anyway. Eventually the two of us would have to talk, but I wasn't ready for that yet.

The next few days passed by in a blur. My heart ached, but somehow I'd managed to convince myself that Jeff and Nina getting back together now was for the best. Better to face it before our baby was here rather than after. I kept rehearsing what I'd say to Jeff when he returned home, praying that when I gave him a piece of my mind I would also manage to maintain my dignity.

Jeff called a few more times during the week, he even tried Facetiming me, but I never mustered the courage to answer. He left a worried message. "I've tried to call you a few times. I know the time difference is brutal, but I hope everything's okay with you and the baby."

By his tone, I assumed that Nina hadn't told him I'd called. If she had, he would've been smart enough to realize that I knew about the two of them which was why I wasn't answering his calls.

When Jeff returned to New York a little over a week after he'd left, his calls increased in frequency. He left a message saying he was back, then another asking if I wanted to meet for dinner, and another demanding I call him back and tell him what the hell was going on and why I wasn't answering my phone. I knew there was only so long I could continue avoiding him, so I finally worked up the courage to answer when he called.

"Why haven't you been picking up your phone?" he asked as soon as I came on the line.

"I'm sorry, but unlike you I don't have anyone to answer my calls for me."

"What is that supposed to mean?" He seemed taken aback by my words.

"I don't know," I said, not even attempting to conceal how hurt I felt. "Why don't you go ask Nina?" I hung up as soon as the words came out, feeling angry, humiliated, and a little ashamed of myself for acting so childishly.

Jeff called right back.

"I don't want to talk to you right now," I said.

"Susan, don't hang up. Tell me what's going on. Why are you so pissed off at me?"

"Why do you even care? You have Nina now; what do you need me for?"

"Nina? What are you talking about?"

I hung up again and threw myself down on the couch, letting the cushions soak up my tears. My phone didn't ring again for a while and when it did, it was Jesse, not Jeff.

"What the heck is going on with you and Jeff?" she said.

"I don't want to talk about it," I replied in the calmest voice I could manage. "Besides, how do you even know anything's going on?"

"He just called me asking if I knew why you were mad at him."

"Seriously? He should know the answer to that."

"Well, he doesn't. The only thing he knows is that it has something to do with Nina," Jesse said. "I told him I didn't know anything, because I don't, which is weird, because you usually call me when something's wrong."

"I can't talk to you about Jeff," I said brusquely, "He's your family, and I'm not."

"Susan, seriously? He might be my brother-in-law, but you're my best friend."

"Well, there's nothing to talk about anyway. Just tell Jeff that I want to be left alone. He can go on living happily ever after with Nina for all I care."

"Jeff and Nina?" Jesse sounded incredulous. "You've got to be kidding me?"

It was a relief that at least Jesse didn't know, because it would've killed me if she did and hadn't said anything. "I know they're back together," I said.

"No way. Jeff hates Nina. He would never get back together with her."

"Really? Then why is she answering his phone? I'm about to have his baby and I don't even do that," I said, trying not to raise my voice. But I was angry, so controlling my temper wasn't the easiest thing to do. I had to remind myself that it wasn't Jesse I was mad at.

"There's got to be an explanation," Jesse insisted.

"Well, whatever it is, I don't care." I knew Jesse was only trying to help, but I was too upset to listen to her try and defend Jeff.

"Sue, you can't mean that."

I didn't feel like talking anymore. "Listen, Jesse. I'm sorry, but I don't want to talk about this. I have to go," I said, and then hung up the phone.

I knew Jesse was probably going to call Jeff and tell him about our conversation. She'd be pissed when Jeff told her the truth—that he'd decided to get back together with Nina. But in the end she'd forgive him, because he was a part of her family. She didn't really have a choice. I needed my best friend to hate the man who'd just broken my heart, but that's not something she could do. And as much as I wanted to keep hating him, I couldn't either. He was my baby's father. I shook my head. How the hell had I gotten myself into this situation?

It felt like the walls of my living room were closing in on me. I needed a break. A break from my shoebox apartment, and the baby stuff piled in the corner of the room, and the bed I'd spent so many nights in with Jeff beside me. I hurriedly stuffed a duffel bag full of clothes, put Bailey's leash around his neck and got on the train, heading to Mom's house. I prayed that the cops wouldn't give me a fine for bringing my dog on the subway, or that my mom wouldn't tell me that Bailey had to stay outside. I was in desperate need of my mom's cooking and pampering, but I didn't want to leave Bailey alone all weekend.

After getting to my mom's, she opened the door and ushered me and Bailey inside without a single complaint about dog hair or dirty paw prints. I headed straight for my old bedroom and threw myself down on the bed crying. I just lay there for a few minutes, letting the bedsheets soak up my tears. After a few minutes I got up, turned off my cell phone and closed the door, thankful that my mom and Frank knew enough to give me the space I needed. Somehow just being away from my apartment, in the home I'd grown up in, was comforting, and having Bailey nestled beside me in my old bed helped ease the pain that had settled in my chest.

But one night wasn't enough to recuperate. In the morning, still not ready to face the world, I stayed inside most of the day, only stepping outside to take Bailey for walks. My mom didn't ask questions, instead she tried cheering me up the best way she knew how—by cooking my favorite dishes. I had no appetite, though.

"You have to think about the baby," Mom said, noticing my untouched plate of food. I managed a few bites, knowing she was right.

I spent a lot of the day in bed and on the couch flipping through channels, pretending not to notice the looks that passed back and forth between my mom and Frank. I knew my mom wanted me to talk to her, but I just couldn't, and I was glad she didn't push.

Close to midnight, just as I was about to doze off, I heard noise coming from the street outside. That wasn't so unusual for a Brooklyn neighborhood. I figured whoever it was they would eventually move on, but when the noise got louder I yanked myself out of bed and walked into the living room, ready to throw the front door open and give Mr. Crazy a piece of my mind. The closer I got to the front of the house, the louder the voice got. Incomprehensible random shouting turned into actual words. It took a moment for what I was hearing to make sense, and when it did I couldn't believe my ears. Jeff was standing outside my mother's house calling my name like a drunken fool.

"Susan, I know you're in there," he bellowed, his speech slurred. "Open the door."

Annoyed, I considered ignoring him and going back to bed until he called my name out again, this time louder. If he kept it up he was going to wake up my mom, Frank, and the neighbors. Not sure what to do, I just stood there. I was half tempted to knock on my mom's door and ask her to tell Jeff I wasn't there, except I didn't want to bother her. But if I told him to go away, then he'd know I really was hiding out at my mom's, and I didn't want that either.

He called my name again. My mother emerged from her bedroom followed by Frank. Jeff's howling had woken them both up and they stalked out of their bedroom looking less than amused.

"What the hell is going on out here?" my mom asked, pulling her bathrobe closed.

"Jeff's here. And I'm pretty sure he's drunk."

My mother crossed the room and unlocked the door.

"What are you doing?" I said.

"Opening the door. If he keeps up that shouting he's going to wake up the neighbors, who are going to call the police and I don't want to have to explain to the entire neighborhood why the cops were at my house in the middle of the night."

"Mom, no," I said as she reached for the doorknob.

"He's the father of your child, Susan. You can't just keep ignoring him and hiding out here. You two are going to be parents soon. It's time you start acting like it."

"Stop that racket and get your *culo* in here," my mom called out to Jeff. She only used bad words in Italian, never in English.

"I'm so sorry, Mrs. Calabro," Jeff said as she closed the door behind him. "I didn't mean to wake you up."

My mom frowned and looked back and forth between the two of us. "C'mon Frank," she finally said, reaching for his hand. "They're grownups, they can sort this out themselves."

Mom headed back to her bedroom with Frank and closed the door behind them. I stood staring at Jeff for a moment before saying, "Well, since you're here, you might as well take a seat."

Silently, he crossed the room and sat down on the sofa.

I crossed my arms and turned to face him. "What the hell do you think you're doing showing up at my mom's house in the middle of the night, drunk and making a fool out of yourself?"

"You wouldn't talk to me, so I didn't have any other choice. I just needed a little liquid courage first."

"A little?" I said, frowning.

Jeff shrugged. "Okay, maybe a lot." He got up from the couch and walked over to me, reaching for my hand. "You're pregnant, you should be the one sitting."

"Just because I'm pregnant doesn't mean I'm fragile. Although I suppose that explains why you didn't want to tell me about Nina. You think I'm too delicate to handle the truth."

"I want you to sit, because you're my girl, and I'm trying to be a gentleman."

Why did Jeff calling me his girl still send my heart fluttering when I knew better? I stared into his eyes. "I'm not your girl."

"You got it all wrong about Nina," Jeff said, shaking his head.

"Jeff, please don't lie to me. I know you want to be a father to our baby. If you're worried that I'll cut you out of his or her life if we're not together, then you can just stop. I won't do that."

"Then why haven't you been returning any of my calls?"

"I just needed some time to get my head together." I refused to confess that it wasn't really my head that needed time, but my heart. I would not tell him how much I loved him and wanted him. Needed him. How hearing Nina's voice on his phone had torn my heart into pieces.

"Nina and I aren't back together," Jeff said, his voice almost a whisper.

"Really?" I asked, my voice full of sarcasm. "Then why was she with you? Why did she answer your phone? A woman doesn't just pick up someone's phone unless they've given her the impression it's okay." Just like Greg's new girl had. He'd probably even asked her to answer my call so I'd know that it was really and truly over between us. Hearing Nina's voice on the phone had been the worst case of deja vu I'd ever had.

Jeff put his hand on my chin, lifting it and forcing me to meet his gaze. "She came by my apartment the afternoon before I left for Singapore, asking for another chance. I told her no. I told her I was with someone else. I even told her about the baby. But she refused to take no for an answer. We were in the middle of arguing when a package came for me, I went downstairs to sign for it, which must have been when you called. I had no idea she answered my phone, or that you'd even called. I thought you were at work."

"I was at work. I called on my lunch break because I wanted to talk to you before you left," I said, softening a little, but still not convinced by his story. "I left a message with her. You never called back."

"Nina never told me you called. She wouldn't have, because if I'd known she answered my phone, I would have been even more furious with her than I already was."

Right. That made sense. More sense than me thinking Nina gave my message to Jeff and he'd chosen to ignore it. I was seriously beginning to feel like a complete idiot. "Why were you furious with her?"

"She showed up completely unannounced. She still had the key to get into the building and came right up to my door like it was no big deal. When I asked her to leave, she refused. I told her that after what she had done to me, it was over between us for good. That's when she broke down and started crying, saying she made the worst mistake of her life when she cheated on me, and that she wanted another chance."

My blood practically boiled at Jeff's words. He was mine, how dare Nina try and weasel her way back into his life after what she'd done?

"I couldn't get her to back off. By the time I finally convinced her to leave, I was running late for my flight. I almost missed it because of her. That's why I wasn't able to call you before I got on the plane."

I looked away, feeling a mixture of relief, regret, and embarrassment. "Jesse told me once that Nina was the love of your life," I said. "I was afraid that you got back together with her and that you didn't want to tell me because of the baby."

Jeff reached for my hand. "I don't have feelings for Nina anymore. Once upon a time I truly believed I loved her, but that was before I knew better," he said. "It was before I met you and realized what love is really supposed to feel like. Nina has never been the love of my life. You are."

I lifted my gaze and stared into Jeff's eyes. "What did you just say?"

He inched closer to me. "I said I love you." His hand came to rest on my cheek. I put mine on top of his.

"That's the first time you've ever said that," I murmured.

"I'm not very good with words. I've always been better at showing my feelings than saying them. Or at least that's what I thought. Apparently I wasn't doing a very good job at that either."

"No, you were," I said, as tears started to streak down my cheeks. "But sometimes a girl just needs things to be said."

Jeff wiped my tears with his thumb. His forehead came to rest on mine for a moment and then he pulled me into a kiss. It was passionate, hungry, and set my heart on a wild rollercoaster ride. And over too soon. Jeff pulled away and looked into my eyes. "I love you, Susan."

"Are you sure you're not just saying that because you're drunk?" I said, trying to hide a smile.

"I'm not drunk," Jeff protested. I gave him a skeptical look. "Tipsy, but not drunk."

"So what now?" I said, still not really sure where all of tonight's revelations left us. Jeff loved me, I loved him, but I'd also hurt him by believing the worst and then not giving him a chance to explain.

"Say you'll come home with me."

"Now? It's the middle of the night."

"You like making me beg, don't you?"

"No, I don't. And you don't need to beg." I rested my hands on his chest. "Because there's nothing I want more than to be with you."

"Careful what you say," Jeff said, his lips curling into a sexy smile. "Because I plan on *being* with you all night."

I gathered my things and left a note for my mom while Jeff called for a cab. With Bailey in tow, the two of us piled into a taxi. It was practically one in the morning by the time we got to Jeff's apartment, but I was wide awake.

The second he closed the door behind us, I turned around and kissed him, edging my tongue inside his mouth, desperate to taste him, drink him, get my fill of him. I didn't even realize how much I'd missed him until he'd shown up at my mom's house.

His coat fell to the floor first, then mine did. There were still too many clothes between us. I wanted to feel his skin on mine. I wanted to run my hands over his naked flesh. Jeff's hands twined through my hair, feeding the fire already blazing in me. "I want you so bad," I whispered in his ear before running my tongue over the skin on his neck. He responded with a soft moan.

We stumbled into the bedroom. I pushed Jeff down on the bed and straddled him. He stared up at me as I removed my bra. He lowered my underwear, then reached up to cup my breasts. I reached for his erection, guiding it inside me, moaning as he slid in and out of me with every thrust. The two of us had been without each other for far too long, it didn't take much time for first me, then Jeff to climax.

"God, I missed you," Jeff finally said as he caught his breath.

"I missed you too," I said before falling silent for a moment. "I'm sorry I believed the worst."

"You're going to have to stop doing that."

"I know." I felt ashamed, remorseful for the way I'd treated him. "But you have to understand that none of this is easy for me. So much has happened. One day I'm engaged and then out of nowhere I'm not. Then you and I hook up and I wind up pregnant with your baby, and I'm sure you won't be happy because you're a player who doesn't want to be tied down. Even after you said I was wrong, that you wanted me, that you were happy about the baby, I couldn't let myself believe it was true."

"Why not?"

"Have you ever seen yourself, Jeff? You're gorgeous."

"You're pretty damn hot yourself, Susan."

I smiled at his compliment. "I'm in my thirties. Most women my age are married with a few kids running around. I'm supposed to want to be with one person, and I'm supposed to want to be a mom. You're only twenty-four. You should be out clubbing and taking a new woman home every night. Like you were doing before I got knocked up."

"That life didn't make me happy. I only acted like it did because that's what people expect," Jeff said. "And just so you know, I'll be twenty-five in another few weeks."

"Great. So then I'll only be seven years older than you."

Jeff chuckled. "You're impossible sometimes, has anyone ever told you that?"

I smiled again and shrugged. "Maybe a few times."

He reached for my hand, lacing his fingers through mine. "I get it, I really do. I understand where you're coming from. But from now on we need to start trusting each other."

The baby started kicking as if he or she were trying to tell me something. I took Jeff's hand and placed it on my belly. "Do you feel that?" I asked.

He smiled. "Our baby is going to be a soccer player."

I turned to look at him, and the happiness etched on his face made my heart skip. I wanted him to be as excited about our baby as I was, and I loved seeing that he was.

"And huge," I said. "I've still got three more months to go, and I'm already as big as a house."

Jeff kissed the top of my head. "You're not big, you're pregnant. And you're beautiful."

I smiled. Jeff pulled me closer so I could snuggle beside him. With his arms wrapped around me I fell asleep, blissfully happy.

Chapter 25
A Promise

In the morning Jeff and I were both way too tired to go to work. We called in sick and enjoyed a long overdue morning of sleeping in together instead. By the time the two of us crawled out of bed it was almost noon. After a shower and breakfast I picked up the pile of clothes we had left scattered on the floor the night before and started packing my things back into my duffel bag.

Jeff walked over to me and grabbed my hand. "Don't go," he said.

I looked up at him and sighed. "Believe me, I don't want to, but I can't miss any more work, and I don't have another change of clothes. Not clean ones, at least."

"Then go home and pack. Bring your clothes here, all of them."

"Jeff, I . . ." Before I could finish what I wanted to say he turned away, walked over to the nightstand, and pulled something out of the drawer.

He turned back around and said, "Just answer one question for me. Why won't you say yes?"

I almost gave him another one of my excuses, but then I remembered how I'd promised him trust. "I want you to want me to move in with you because you love me, because you want to be with me, not because you think it's right for the baby." After the huge misunderstanding we'd just had I owed it to Jeff to be honest, no matter how hard it was to confess my feelings.

"Can't I want you to move in for both reasons?"

"If I weren't pregnant would you be asking?"

"Yes, yes I would. Because I love you. When you're not here, this place feels empty and I'm half-tempted to get up in the middle of the night, go to Brooklyn, and pound on your door. You're fun and you're funny, you're sweet and caring and sexy as hell, and I know I won't ever feel this way for any other woman in the world."

"Sexy?" I glanced down at my gigantic belly. "Like this?"

"Yes, even pregnant you're the most beautiful woman I've ever seen," Jeff said. "The one I want to spend the rest of my life with."

He got down on one knee in front of me and opened his hand, the one that had been clenched around what he'd taken from his drawer. My heart flipped, somersaulted, and did some sort of crazy high dive in my chest. This could not be happening.

"What are you doing?" I asked when I finally caught my breath.

"Exactly what it looks like," Jeff opened the small, black velvet box in his hands, revealing a diamond ring resting inside. He held it up to me. "Susan, will you marry me?"

I didn't even know it was possible to feel like fainting and jumping for joy at the same time. I took his hands and pulled him up. When he was on his feet I practically fell into his arms. My knees had turned to jelly. "Yes, Jeff. I'll marry you," I said, my voice trembling.

He took a step back from me, and glanced down at Bailey who was curled up on top of the bed. "You are my witness, Bailey." At the sound of his name Bailey's head lifted. "She said yes." Jeff turned his attention back to me. With a smile on his face and that sparkle in his eyes that I loved so much he said, "You're sure that you want to marry me? You're not just saying yes because of the baby?"

I couldn't contain my laughter. "Well," I said with a shrug, "I can't really be sure."

He laughed right back and wrapped his arms around me. "No more joking this time. Do you really want to do this?"

I nodded and kissed him. "Only if you promise me something."

"Anything."

"I don't want to walk down the aisle wearing a maternity wedding dress."

"What are you saying? That you want to wait until after the baby comes?" Jeff seemed surprised. He probably figured I wanted to be married before our baby was born.

"Mmm hmm."

"That's fine with me. As long as I get you down the aisle before his or her first birthday."

"Oh, you will," I said before reaching around the nape of Jeff's neck and pulling him into a kiss. It didn't take long for the two of us to shed the clothes we'd just gotten dressed in and make our way back in bed.

A few hours later Jeff, Bailey, and I headed over to my apartment. He helped me pack a few bags and then the three of us turned right back around and returned to his place.

Because work kept us both busy until the weekend, we waited until then to move the rest of my stuff from the apartment in Brooklyn I'd lived in for the past seven years. Saturday morning the two of us drove over in a small U-Haul rental. While Jeff parked it in an empty spot on the street I fished my keys out of my purse. As I lifted my head to open the truck door I noticed Jesse and Justin waiting by the door to my building.

"What are you two doing here?" I asked, walking over to them.

Jesse gave me a quick hug. "Helping you move." After dropping her arms from around me, she reached for my hand, the one that wore the ring Jeff had given me. "Oh my God, Susan, your ring is so beautiful."

It really was pretty. Jeff had bought it in Singapore, planning to propose when he returned. The ring was simple, but elegant; a round cut, bezel set diamond on a platinum band. Ever since Jeff had put it on my finger I couldn't stop myself from glancing at it every few minutes.

Justin hugged me next. "You do know what this means, right?" he said.

"What what means?"

"The four of us are going to be family." His words warmed my heart. "Congratulations," he said.

"Are we going to stand out here hugging each other all other day?" Jeff teased. "Because I don't know about the rest of you, but I'm freezing."

I tugged on Jeff's hand, unlocked the door and led him up the stairs with Jesse and Justin trailing behind us. After we were all inside, I pulled Jeff into the kitchen. "When did you tell them? And more importantly why didn't you wait for me so we could share the news together?"

"I kind of couldn't, because I told Justin a few weeks ago that I was planning on asking you to marry me after I got back from Singapore. He kept bugging me all week to tell him what you said."

I looked down at my ring, still surprised that I was actually engaged. "I can't believe this is really happening. A few weeks ago I thought I'd lost you for good."

Jeff shook his head. "Let's not think about that anymore."

"Hey you two lovebirds," Justin called, "are you going to tell us what to do, or are we just supposed to stand around here while you two make out in the kitchen?"

I peered around the doorway into the living room, grinning. "We are not making out."

Jeff refused to let me lift anything heavy. Justin and Jesse backed him up when I protested, so Jesse and I filled boxes while Jeff and his brother carried them down the stairs. My furniture was staying because Jeff's was much nicer than mine and we didn't need two couches. It took only a few hours to empty my place of everything I wanted to take with me.

We headed back into the city and unloaded my stuff. Jeff and I filled the second bedroom with the baby gifts I'd kept in the corner of my living room. I couldn't wait for the two of us to set up the crib and decorate the room.

All that packing and unpacking left us hungry. After we were finished, the four of us went out to dinner to celebrate. Later, after Jesse and Justin left, I decided it was time to call my mom and tell her my news.

"Well, this is certainly an unexpected turn," she said, "but I'm happy for you. Even if it means I'll have to go all the way to the city to visit."

"It's not that much farther."

"I know, I'm just giving you a hard time, because that's what mothers do," she said. "Have the two of you set a date?"

"Not quite. I was thinking some time in the early fall when it's not hot anymore would be nice. I'd really like a small outside wedding."

"Did you just say small? You may be my only child, but you've got a ton of cousins, and they're all going to expect an invitation."

"I know, but how am I going to plan a giant wedding like that while I'm taking care of a newborn?"

"That's what wedding planners are for," my mother said.

"Mom, wedding planners are expensive."

"Don't worry about money. You're my only child. Let's just say I've been saving up for this occasion for a long time."

I wanted to protest and tell my mother to spend that money on herself, but I knew I'd never get her to change her mind. Instead I thanked her and told her how much I loved and appreciated her.

"I'm just happy that I can do this for you," my mom said.

Truthfully, I was happy too, because before I walked down any aisles, I had boxes full of unpacking to do, a baby shower that was coming up in a few weeks, and scariest of all, a baby to give birth to.

Chapter 26
Arrival

The next few months seemed to fly by. Jeff and I decorated the baby's bedroom, picking neutral colors for the boy or girl we were soon going to have. We put the crib together ourselves and moved it into the corner of the room. A rocking chair and changing table filled the rest of the space.

Thirty-two weeks into my pregnancy, Jesse threw a baby shower that neither Jeff nor I would ever forget. Our friends and family gave us so many presents that by the time my water broke six weeks later I was sure we were as ready as two people could possibly be to bring a baby into the world.

It was a hot and humid day in early July. After my water broke, I called Dr. Lu, who told me to grab the bag I'd packed and get myself to the hospital. As soon as I got off the phone with her my contractions started. During childbirth classes, the instructor had explained that labor pains felt like strong menstrual cramps. It didn't sound so bad at the time, but as my contractions became more intense, I began to realize she'd been grossly understating their severity.

I'd been on maternity leave for the past week, but Jeff was

still working. I called him, praying that he wasn't in the middle of a meeting because I wanted him beside me, holding my hand while I gave birth to our baby.

"My water just broke," I said as soon as he answered.

"Are you serious?"

A contraction hit and I remembered my breathing, but not before groaning from the pain.

"Oh my God," he said, sounding panicked, "you're in labor? Right now?"

"Yes, Jeff." I took another deep breath. "Right now."

"Can you wait for me? I'm going to leave the office right now. I'll be there as fast as I can."

"I can wait. But hurry."

After Jeff made it home, we piled into a taxi. I texted Jesse, asking her to make sure Bailey got fed and walked.

She texted back. *I'm so excited!!! I'm going to be an aunt!!!*

Jeff held my hand as the taxi drove us into Brooklyn and toward the hospital I had planned to give birth in. The contractions got stronger and more frequent.

"Are you sure she's going to be okay, sir?" the driver asked Jeff nervously. "She's not going to give birth in here, is she?"

"No, no, of course not," he replied.

Jeff leaned in and whispered in my ear, "You're not, are you?"

I scowled at him. "No. I better not."

Thankfully, I did not give birth in the back of the taxi cab. After arriving at the hospital I got checked in, changed into one of those hideous gowns, had my blood drawn and an IV started, and then just waited. Even though my contractions were coming every few minutes, I was nowhere near fully dilated. The pain became too much for me, and I asked for an epidural. As the pain subsided I relaxed a bit, and a few hours later, with Jeff beside me, I gave birth to an almost-nine-pound baby boy.

The craziest feeling of bliss came over me as Dr. Lu placed him in my arms for the first time. Tears of joy trickled down my face as Jeff and I stared down in awe at the baby we had never intended to make.

"He's amazing," Jeff kept saying over and over.

The nurse came to take him from me so he could be weighed and examined. "So do you two have a name for this little guy?"

Jeff and I looked at each other. "We picked out a name for a girl, but nothing for a boy," I told her.

After the nurse finished her exam she handed our son back to me, swaddled, and with a hat covering his fine brown hair. She left me and Jeff alone in the room.

"So what do you think he looks like?" I asked Jeff as I stared at our baby's beautiful face.

"What about Zachary?" Jeff suggested. "I've always liked that name."

Maybe it was the hormones, or the joy of holding my baby in my arms after so many months, but the name sounded perfect to me. "Zachary Lambert." I stroked his soft little cheek with my fingertip. "Welcome to this crazy world."

Epilogue
Three Months Later

Almost a year after Jeff and I spent our first night together following Jesse and Justin's wedding, we walked down the aisle and exchanged our vows. I held little Zachary in my arms during the ceremony, only handing him to my mom when the wedding officiant instructed Jeff to place the ring on my finger.

Our wedding was held at the historic Picnic House in Prospect Park, Brooklyn. Despite being in a big city, it felt like we were actually in an intimate private garden. The spectacular red, yellow, and orange autumn leaves provided a beautiful backdrop to the wedding canopy, decorated with greenery and white flowers. It was the wedding I'd always dreamed of having. Not only was the venue gorgeous, and the weather perfect, but I got to walk down the aisle in a dress that made me feel like a princess. It was cap-sleeved, with a bodice decorated in lace and beads and a full tulle skirt. But what made my wedding day so magical was Jeff, and our baby, and each and every family member and friend that clapped after we kissed for the first time as husband and wife.

Zach was three months old. He had my crazy wavy hair and

Jeff's beautiful blue eyes. I loved everything about him from his chunky thighs to his adorable dimples. He still woke up every few hours at night, demanding to be held and fed. As tired as I was, whenever I looked down at him in my arms, my heart swelled. Despite being seriously sleep deprived, I had never been happier in my entire life.

Jeff made a wonderful partner. A few weeks before our baby was born he'd asked if I'd thought about whether or not I wanted to go back to work. I agonized over the decision. I'd put so much energy into getting my education degree, that I just couldn't imagine walking away from all the hard work I'd put in. But I wanted time with my baby, too.

After Zach was born, the decision became easy. I didn't want to be apart from him. I wanted to be the one who took care of him and nurtured him. The one who fed him, put him down for naps, and yes, even the one who changed his diapers. Jeff supported my decision to stay home. And while I still felt frazzled from time to time, I relished my role as a mother.

Zach had turned both my life and Jeff's upside-down. But we loved our crazy life. It was because of Zach that we decided to have an afternoon wedding instead of an evening one. So we could end the day putting him down to sleep in his crib. Having a baby changed the way we did everything; it affected so many decisions, but our lives were richer for it.

After the ceremony, our wedding reception began. Zach had so many loving arms to hold him while Jeff and I enjoyed our fancy catered lunch, cut our gorgeous three-tiered cake that had been decorated with real flowers, and partied.

"We're cutting in," Jesse said as she walked up to us holding

Justin's hand. Jeff and I had been in the middle of dancing to one of our favorite songs.

Justin reached for my hand. "Congratulations, Sue, I'm so glad you and my brother found each other," he said as the two of us danced. "You two make almost as perfect a couple as me and Jess."

"Jesse told me about you trying to play matchmaker," I said, smiling. "I wasn't so happy about it at the time, but now I'm glad you did."

"She thought it was a bad idea. I think she worried that Jeff would hurt you, but I know my brother better than anyone else, which is how I knew the two of you would be perfect together," he said. "Besides, I saw the way he looked at you during me and Jesse's wedding shower. You made him smile."

"Well then, I only have one thing to say."

Justin raised his eyebrows. "And that would be?"

"Thank you for ignoring your wife," I said.

By the time our reception came to an end, I was tired and my feet ached from all the dancing I'd done. Jeff and I returned home in our rented limousine. Little Zach fell asleep on the way and continued his nap while Jeff and I changed out of our wedding attire. After, we sat beside each other on the couch while Zach slept in his Pack 'N Play.

"Have I told you how happy I am?" Jeff asked, taking one of my feet in his hands to massage it.

"Are you? Even though we aren't headed for a romantic honeymoon in the Caribbean?"

"That can wait until Zach's older. And you know I'm just as happy being here in our apartment with you, Zach, and Bailey."

I smiled. "Have I told you how much I love you?"

Jeff leaned toward me. "You have, but I never get tired of hearing it."

I wrapped my arms around him and pulled him closer, teasing him with kisses that were way too polite for a newlywed couple. "I love you, Jeff Lambert."

He pressed his lips on mine, pushing his tongue into my mouth, demanding more from the woman who'd just become his wife. "Not as much as I love you, Susan Lambert."

We glanced at Zach, who was still fast asleep. Bailey lay on the floor curled up beside the play yard. From the moment we'd brought Zach home, Bailey had taken to him. He often slept right beside him at the foot of his crib or bouncy chair.

Jeff lifted me into his arms. "What if he wakes up?" I asked.

"He won't. He knows his mom and dad just got married. We're only ever going to have one wedding day, and I plan on making love to my wife on it."

I returned the smile that he gave me. "Then what are you waiting for?"

"Nothing, my love, nothing," he said as he carried me into our bedroom to make love to me for the first time as husband and wife.

Want to be notified when Teresa Roman's next book will be released? Then sign up for her mailing list by going to http://eepurl.com/bSYLZr. Your email address will never be shared and you can unsubscribe at any time.

Word of mouth and reviews are essential for an author's success. If you enjoyed this book, please consider leaving a review. Even a short review would be helpful and greatly appreciated.

Thank you.

Connect with me online.
Website: www.teresaromanwrites.com
Facebook: www.facebook.com/teresaromanauthor
Twitter: www.twitter.com/TRomanauthor
Goodreads: www.goodreads.com/author/show/14163515.Teresa_Roman
Instagram: www.instagram.com/teresaromanauthor/

Also by Teresa Roman:

Back to Us
Daughter of Magic
Legacy

Acknowledgements

First off, I'd like to thank my beautiful children. The path to motherhood is different for everyone, but once you get there, life is never the same. I also want to thank my little sister, who has been more than just a sibling for as long as I can remember. She has been my family and my best friend, my shoulder to cry on and my cheerleader. I can't imagine life without her. A big thank you also goes out to my amazing editor, Jennifer Skutelsky. Last, but not definitely not least, I want to thank each and every person who read this book. It means the world to me that out of the millions of books out there, you chose to read mine.

About the Author

Teresa Roman writes contemporary and paranormal romance for adults and young adults. If it was possible to be born with a book in her hands, that's how Teresa Roman would've entered this world. Her passion for reading is what inspired her to become a writer. She loves the way stories can take you to another time and place.

Born in Romania, Teresa has lived in the Midwest and on both coasts, but currently calls Sacramento, CA her home. She lives there with her husband, three adorable children and a dog named Parker that her son convinced them to adopt. When she's not at her day job or running around with her kids, you can find her in front of the computer writing, or with her head buried in another book.

www.ingramcontent.com/pod-product-compliance
Lightning Source LLC
Chambersburg PA
CBHW021011120726
47905CB00009B/2954